THREADS OF MEMORY

THREAD WITCH BOOK 1

ALSO BY RICHARD FIERCE

DRAGON RIDERS OF OSNEN

Trial by Sorcery
A Bond of Flame
The Warrior's Call
The Coin of Souls
Wings of Terror
Eyes of Stone
Tooth and Claw
The Servant of Souls
Smoke and Shadow
The Dark Rider
The Song of Bones
Sword and Crown
Tides of Darkness
Wrath and Ruin
Tomb of Oaths

MARKED BY THE DRAGON

Curse of the Dragon
Scale of the Dragon
Egg of the Dragon
Call of the Dragon
Wrath of the Dragon
Sacrifice of the Dragon

THREADS OF MEMORY

THREAD WITCH BOOK 1

RICHARD FIERCE

Dragonfire Press

Print ISBN: 979-8-89631-089-1

To my readers.
Thank you for everything.

THREAD WITCH
1
THREADS OF MEMORY
RICHARD FIERCE

CHAPTER 1
Amara

They say cloth remembers the dead. Amara knew better. Cloth didn't just remember, it *spoke.*

The morning fog clung to Deymar's market like a shroud, muffling the cries of merchants hawking their wares. Amara pulled her worn shawl tighter around her shoulders and surveyed the torn cloak spread across her workbench. The fabric was coarse military wool, dyed the deep crimson of House Valdris, but the color had faded to the rust of dried blood. Three jagged tears ran through the chest—claw marks, by the look of them.

"Beast got him good," muttered the soldier who'd brought it to her stall. He came to her often enough that she knew he favored his left leg and had a wife who embroidered roses on his handkerchiefs. "Captain wore that cloak through seven campaigns. Shame to see him find an end like this."

Amara's fingers traced the tears, feeling the weight of memory settled into the wool like sediment. The cloak had absorbed years of sweat, smoke, and fear. She could sense it all—the thunder of hooves, the clash of steel, the sharp coppery taste of blood. Most seamstresses would simply patch the holes and charge three coppers for the work. But Amara was not most seamstresses.

"I'll have it ready by evening," she said, not meeting the soldier's eyes. Around them, the market churned with its daily commerce: fishmongers shouting over baskets of silver-scaled catch, children dodging between cart wheels, goodwives fingering bolts of cheap cotton. None of them paid attention to the quiet woman with the mending stall tucked between the cheese seller and the tinker.

That was how Amara preferred it.

The soldier dropped four coppers on her bench—twice her usual fee. "Captain always said his cloak would keep fighting even after he was gone. Mad old bastard." His voice cracked slightly. "Make it right, seamstress. He deserves that much."

After he left, Amara sorted through her basket of threads, selecting a deep crimson that would blend with the faded wool. Her needle was nothing special—plain steel, worn smooth by years of use. No rune-etched silver like the Guild weavers carried. No mystical properties beyond the skill in her hands and the gift she'd never asked for.

She began to stitch, her movements precise and practiced. With each draw of the needle, the tear grew smaller. But as the wool knitted itself back together, something else stirred in the fabric. A whisper, faint as wind through autumn leaves.

Formation seven... shield wall... watch the left flank...

Amara's hands stilled. The voice was not her own—it rose from the cloak like smoke from dying embers. She glanced around quickly, but the market crowd continued its business, oblivious to the phantom words.

They're breaking through. Sound the retreat... no, hold the line. Hold—

The voice grew clearer, more insistent. The captain, speaking from the realm the dead inhabited, his commands threading themselves through the wool that had sheltered him in life. Amara's needle trembled.

This was what she feared most. Not the Guild's laws against unlicensed weaving, not the whispered rumors of thread-witches who could trap souls in cloth. She feared the moment when her gift would announce itself to the world, when she could no longer pretend to be just another seamstress mending holes for copper coins.

"I said hold the line!" The voice cracked like a whip, and several people in the nearby stalls turned their heads, searching for its source.

Amara's breath caught. She pressed her palm flat against the cloak, trying to muffle the spirit's words, but it was too late. A woman at the cheese stall had gone pale, pointing at Amara with a shaking finger.

"Thread-witch," the woman hissed. "She's awakened something in the cloth."

The word rippled through the market like a stone thrown into still water. Conversations died. Merchants stepped back from their stalls. A child tugged at his mother's skirt, asking why the soldier's voice was coming from the cloak.

Amara's hands moved frantically, trying to finish the repairs and silence the ghostly captain, but her haste made her clumsy. The needle slipped, pricking her thumb. A drop of blood fell onto the wool, and Captain Thorne's voice roared to life with terrible clarity.

"Form ranks! The enemy comes from the north! Gods save us, they've brought the siege engines! All men to the—"

The phantom words cut off abruptly as Amara completed the final stitch and yanked her hands away from the cloak. The sudden silence was deafening. Every eye in the market square was fixed on her stall, faces twisted with fear, suspicion, and in some cases, hunger.

She knew that look. It was the same expression worn by those who would use her gift—nobles seeking to commune with dead lovers, generals wanting to question fallen enemies, the desperate hoping to pull one last secret from a corpse's clothing.

The silence that followed hung heavy over the market square, suffocating Amara like a thick wool blanket. She could feel the weight of every gaze on her, accusatory and fearful, burning into her skin like hot coals.

Amara's heart hammered in her chest, each beat echoing in her ears louder than the ghostly captain's commands. She had tried so hard to keep her gift hidden, to live a quiet life among the bustling stalls of the market. But now, exposed before the prying eyes of the crowd, she felt like a deer surrounded by hungry wolves.

With trembling hands, Amara gathered the repaired cloak, folding it carefully to hide the lingering echoes trapped within its fibers. She knew she had crossed a threshold from which there was no turning back. The revelation of her gift was a beacon calling out to those who would seek to exploit it for their own purposes... or worse, the Guild would send its enforcers after her.

Amara's hands shook as she hastily packed up her mending tools, her heart racing. The weight of the crowd's collective gaze bore down on her, making it hard to think. Fear and uncertainty gripped her, twisting in her gut. She glanced around, searching for an escape route, but the market stalls seemed to have closed in around her, trapping her like a cornered animal.

A sudden commotion at the edge of the market square drew her attention. Through the parting crowd strode a figure clad in black, the distinctive cloak of the Hemlock Circle billowing behind him like a shadow given form.

He was tall and lean, with the wiry strength of someone who'd spent years training for combat. Dark brown hair was in windblown disarray, as though he'd woken up and hadn't bothered to smooth it down. Faint stubble shadowed his jaw, giving him a worn, travel-weathered look that spoke of too many nights on the road.

But it was his eyes that made Amara's breath catch. Steel gray, piercing as winter frost, they swept across the market square with the keen attention of a hawk searching for its prey. Those eyes missed nothing—not the frightened faces of the merchants, not the child clutching his mother's skirts, not the way Amara's hand had frozen above her mending basket. They were calculating eyes, weighing and measuring everything they touched, and when they finally settled on her, Amara felt as though she'd been stripped bare, all her secrets laid out for examination.

Amara's throat went dry. She thought of the basement room where she lived, of the few possessions that marked her small place in the world. She thought of the soldier, who would return for his captain's cloak and find her gone. Most of all, she thought of the needle in her hand—unremarkable to look at, but the instrument of a power that terrified those who understood its implications.

She needed to run, but where? There was nowhere the Guild didn't have a presence. The Unraveler pushed through the crowd, his hand resting on the silver thread-cutter at his belt. "Seamstress," he called, his voice carrying the authority of one who served the Loommaster. "You will come with me."

The crowd pressed closer, forming a circle around her stall. Someone in the back shouted for the city watch, but Amara didn't know why. The guards would do nothing to stop the black-clad man.

Life as she knew it was over. She looked down at the repaired cloak, perfect now except for the faintest shimmer in the wool where her stitches had bound something more than fabric together. Then she looked up at the man, at the fearful faces surrounding her, and made a choice that would change the fate of kingdoms.

"I'll come," she said, setting down her needle with steady hands. "I have nothing to hide."

The Unraveler's eyes watched her every movement as she grabbed the cloak, her movements deliberate and unhurried. Let them think her compliant. Let them believe they had captured just another rogue seamstress.

As she tucked the cloak under her arm and stepped out from behind her stall, the whispers followed her—threads of rumor that would spread through the city like wildfire. By evening, everyone in Deymar would know what happened to her.

"Before you take me to the Guild Hall, I need to return this to my customer."

CHAPTER 2
Caedric

Caedric had been tracking rogue weavers for seven years, and he could spot them from across a crowded square. They all had the same tells—the way their fingers moved when they thought no one was watching, tracing patterns in the air. The unconscious habit of touching fabric as if testing its memory. The careful distance they kept from anything that might betray their gift.

The seamstress walking ahead of him displayed none of these signs, and that made him more suspicious, not less.

She was young—early twenties, perhaps—with dark, wavy hair pulled back in a simple braid that was already beginning to fray in the market's humidity. Loose tendrils curled at her temples and the nape of her neck, giving her an air of gentle disorder despite her obvious attempts at neatness. Her skin had the warm, bronze tone of someone who spent hours working near windows, catching whatever natural light she could for her detailed work. Her hands were lean and strong, marked with the telltale calluses of needlework: small white scars dotting her fingertips like constellations of old pinpricks.

She wasn't delicate, not in the way noble ladies were delicate. Her build suggested someone accustomed to physical labor, someone who hauled bolts of fabric and bent over a workbench for hours without complaint. There was a groundedness to her movements, a steady competence that spoke of years spent mastering an honest trade.

Nothing about her suggested power beyond the ability to mend torn seams. Yet dozens of witnesses had heard a dead man's voice rise from the fabric she'd been stitching.

"Tell me about the man who owned the cloak," Caedric said, matching her steady pace through the crowded lanes.

"I never knew him." Amara's voice was calm, controlled. "The soldier who brought me the cloak said he died fighting some manner of beast."

"Yet his voice spoke through the wool you were mending."

She glanced at him sideways, and for a moment he caught sight of her eyes—deep brown, flecked with gold. Beautiful, he realized with unwelcome surprise. He forced himself to look away, focusing instead on the silver thread-cutter at his belt. Attraction was a luxury he couldn't afford, not when duty demanded his complete attention.

"The crowd was frightened," Amara said. "Fear makes people hear things that aren't there."

"I spoke to three witnesses. They all heard the same words."

"Then perhaps the captain's spirit lingers in the market square, not in his cloak."

Clever, Caedric thought. She deflects without denying, admits nothing while explaining everything. Either she was innocent, or she was better trained than most rogues he'd encountered.

They found the soldier at a tavern near the military quarter. He was deep in his cup, drowning the grief had driven him to pay double for mending a dead man's cloak. Amara approached his table with the careful deference of one who knew her place. "Your captain's cloak, as promised."

The soldier looked up with bleary eyes, then focused on the black-cloaked figure looming behind her. His face went pale. Everyone in Auralis knew what the dark fabric meant—the Hemlock Circle, enforcers of the Guild's will, hunters of those who dared practice the forbidden arts.

"Is there... trouble?" the soldier's voice cracked.

"No trouble," Caedric said, though his tone suggested otherwise. "Simply ensuring your property was returned."

The soldier unfolded the cloak with reverent hands. The tears were gone, the fabric whole once more. But as he held it up to the tavern's lamplight, Caedric watched for any sign of supernatural activity. A whisper, a shimmer, the faintest echo of the voice that had rung out in the market.

Nothing.

The seamstress had done exactly what she claimed—mended torn cloth and nothing more.

"It's perfect," the soldier breathed. "Just like new." He pressed his face into the wool for a moment, then looked up at Amara with grateful eyes. "Thank you. The captain... he would have been pleased."

Caedric studied the man's face, searching for any sign that he heard phantom voices or felt ghostly presences. He showed only the quiet satisfaction of someone whose treasured possession had been restored.

"We should go," Caedric said to Amara. The questioning would continue at the Guild Hall, where proper techniques could be employed.

The local Guild Hall occupied a converted manor house in Deymar's merchant district, its windows fitted with iron bars worked into decorative patterns. To most citizens, it looked like nothing more than another administrative building. But Caedric knew the true purpose of those bars—they were woven with null-thread, designed to contain any supernatural energies that might be unleashed during interrogations.

He led Amara through the main hall, past clerks copying requisitions and archivists cataloguing bolts of sanctioned fabric. None of them looked up. In the Hemlock Circle, discretion was as valued as skill with a thread-cutter.

The questioning room was sparse—a wooden table, two chairs, and a cabinet filled with test materials. Caedric gestured for Amara to sit, then took the chair across from her. Between them lay a selection of cloth samples: a child's nightgown, a merchant's coat, a soldier's glove. Each piece carefully chosen for the strength of memory it might contain.

"State your name and occupation," he began, pulling out a ledger to record her answers.

"Amara Souster. Seamstress."

Caedric's pen paused. "Souster? Like the mayor?"

"A common name in these parts. No relation that I'm aware of."

"How long have you been practicing your trade?"

"Eight years. I learned from my grandmother before she passed."

"And your grandmother—was she Guild-licensed?"

"She was a simple seamstress, nothing more."

The questions continued, each one designed to probe for gaps in her story or hints of hidden knowledge. Caedric had conducted hundreds of such interrogations, and he knew all the tells: nervous laughter, fidgeting hands, the way guilty parties' eyes darted toward whatever they were trying to conceal.

Amara displayed none of these signs. She answered each question directly, her voice steady, her hands folded calmly in her lap. If not for the incident in the market, he would have released her within minutes.

"Pick up the nightgown," he commanded.

She reached for the small garment without hesitation, lifting it with the same professional assessment she'd shown the captain's cloak. The cotton was soft, well-worn, stained with years of childhood dreams and fears.

"What do you feel?" Caedric watched her face intently.

"Cotton. Good quality, but old. The stitching is hand-done, probably by the child's mother."

"Nothing else?"

"Should I feel something else?"

He leaned forward. "Some people claim cloth holds memories. That skilled hands can awaken what lies dormant in the weave."

"People claim many things." Amara set down the nightgown. "I deal in fabric and thread, nothing more."

For the next hour, Caedric tested her with each sample. The merchant's coat that had absorbed decades of calculated greed. The soldier's glove that had drawn blood in three different wars. A nobleman's handkerchief that had wiped away tears of both joy and sorrow.

With each test, Amara remained unmoved. No voices rose from the cloth. No phantoms stirred in the weave. She examined each piece with the detached professionalism of someone evaluating thread count and dye quality, nothing more.

By the time the afternoon light began to fade through the barred windows, Caedric was forced to acknowledge defeat. Whatever had happened in the market, he had no evidence of wrongdoing. No proof of unlicensed weaving. No grounds to hold her further.

"You're free to go," he said finally, closing his ledger with more force than necessary.

Amara stood, smoothing her skirts. "Am I to understand that this interrogation was based solely on rumors and superstition?"

"The Guild takes all reports of unauthorized magical activity seriously."

"I see." She moved toward the door, then paused. "For what it's worth, Unraveler, I understand you were simply doing your duty. I hold no ill will."

The words were polite, even gracious. But as she spoke them, Caedric caught something in her expression—a flicker of amusement, perhaps, or challenge. As if she knew she had bested him and was too polite to say so directly.

He watched her leave, noting the confident set of her shoulders, the unhurried pace of someone with nothing to hide. Or someone very good at hiding it.

When the door closed behind her, Caedric sat alone in the questioning room, staring at the fabric samples spread across the table. Seven years of hunting rogues, and he'd never encountered anyone quite like her. Most unlicensed weavers were driven by desperation or ambition, their gifts raw and uncontrolled. They made mistakes, left evidence, betrayed themselves through arrogance or fear.

Amara had done none of these things.

He stood and walked to the window, peering through the null-thread bars at the street below. She was already gone, vanished into the evening crowd like smoke dissipating in the wind.

But Caedric had not risen to his position in the Hemlock Circle by accepting convenient explanations. The incident in the market had been real—too many witnesses, too many consistent details. Captain Thorne's voice had spoken from that cloak, as surely as if the man himself had been standing there.

Which meant Amara was either the most skilled rogue he'd ever encountered, or something else entirely. Something the Guild's training had never prepared him for.

Either way, he would be watching.

Caedric gathered the test fabrics, returning them to their protective cases. Tomorrow he would file his report, officially closing the investigation with a finding of insufficient evidence. But unofficially, privately, he would keep Amara under surveillance.

It was his duty as an Unraveler, he told himself. Nothing more than professional thoroughness.

The fact that her gold-flecked eyes had haunted him throughout the interrogation was simply an unfortunate complication—one he would learn to ignore, as he had learned to ignore so many other inconvenient truths in service to the Guild.

Outside, the evening bells began to toll, their bronze voices echoing across the city. Somewhere in those twisting streets, a seamstress was returning to her quiet life, secure in the belief that she had escaped notice.

She was wrong.

The hunt was far from over.

CHAPTER 3
Amara

The market felt different now, as if Amara walked through a world made of glass that might shatter at any moment. Conversations died as she passed, only to resume in urgent whispers once she'd moved beyond earshot. The baker who had always nodded politely now studied his loaves with sudden intensity. The florist turned her back entirely, busying herself with arrangements that needed no tending.

But others watched her with a different kind of attention. Hungry eyes followed her movement through the stalls, calculating gazes that weighed her worth like merchants appraising silk. A well-dressed woman in noble house colors lingered near the spice vendor, her fingers worrying the black mourning band on her sleeve. An old man clutched a bundle that might have been clothing, his rheumy eyes never leaving Amara's face.

They knew. Or suspected. Either way, her quiet life of mending torn seams for copper coins was over.

Amara kept her pace steady, her expression neutral, even as her skin crawled under the weight of so much scrutiny. Somewhere among the crowd, she was certain the Unraveler watched as well. She couldn't see him—Caedric was too skilled for that—but she could feel his presence like a cold wind at her back.

Why did he let me go? The question had haunted her through every step from the Guild Hall. She'd given him nothing, revealed nothing, yet his pale eyes had studied her with the intensity of someone reading a book written in a language he didn't quite understand. Men like him didn't release their quarry without reason.

Unless he wanted her to lead him somewhere. Or to someone.

The thought made her quicken her step, turning down the narrow lane that led to her lodgings. Behind her, the market's whispers faded to a dull murmur, but she knew the rumors would spread like ink through water.

Amara's basement room crouched beneath a tailor's shop like a secret waiting to be discovered. The ceiling was so low she had to duck when moving between her bed and worktable, and the single window sat level with the street, offering views of passing boots and not much else. But it was hers, and it was hidden, and until today that had been enough.

She lit the oil lamp with hands that trembled only slightly, pushing back the gathering dusk. Her sewing table held the familiar chaos of her trade: spools of thread in every color, scraps of fabric sorted by weight and weave, the small collection of needles that were her most precious possessions.

In the corner sat a cedar chest that had belonged to her grandmother—the woman who'd taught her that fabric could hold more than shape, more than warmth. Amara knelt beside it now, lifting the lid to reveal carefully folded layers of memory.

At the very bottom lay a square of blue silk, no larger than a child's handkerchief.

Her grandmother's wedding veil, cut down and preserved through decades of hardship. Amara lifted it with reverent hands, feeling the weight of love and loss woven into its delicate threads.

She could awaken it. One careful stitch, and her grandmother's voice would rise from the silk like incense from a shrine. But that wasn't what she needed now.

Instead, Amara threaded her plainest needle with ordinary cotton and began to work. Not to wake, but to silence. Not to bind memory into form, but to wrap it so tightly in new thread that even she couldn't call it forth.

The stitches were tiny, almost invisible, each one placed with the precision of a master craftswoman. But this was harder work than awakening—it required her to press against the fabric's natural tendency to remember, to muffle voices that wanted to sing.

With each stitch, the silk grew quieter. The whispers that lived in its weave—her grandmother's laughter, her wedding day tears, the last words she'd spoken before the fever took her—all of it faded until only ordinary fabric remained.

The effort left Amara gasping. Her fingers cramped, and when she looked down, tiny drops of blood welled from her fingertips like dew. She hadn't noticed the needle slips, too focused on her work to register the small betrayals of flesh.

She realized it wasn't just needle marks. It was threadburn, a sign she'd overused her ability. *This is what it costs,* she thought, wrapping the silk carefully and returning it to the chest. *Every use of the gift takes something from me.*

The Guild would kill her if they knew the truth. Not for practicing unlicensed magic— that was merely illegal. They'd kill her because her gift bypassed their carefully hoarded rune-thread, made mockery of their monopoly on memory-weaving. She could do with plain cotton what their most skilled masters required silver sigils to accomplish.

A sharp knock at her door shattered the silence like a stone through glass.

Amara froze, her heart hammering against her ribs. The Guild? Impossible— she'd only just left their custody. But who else would come calling at this hour?

The knock came again, more insistent. A woman's voice, thick with tears: "Please, I know you're in there. I see the light."

Against her better judgment, Amara cracked the door open. A middle-aged woman stood in the narrow stairwell, her merchants' clothes wrinkled and her eyes red with weeping. In her arms, she clutched a bundle of white cotton—a child's nightgown, by the size of it.

"You're the seamstress from the market," the woman said. It wasn't a question. "The one who can... who can wake the dead."

"I think you're mistaken—"

"Please." The word came out as a broken sob. "My daughter. She passed three days ago from the fever. This is her favorite nightdress, the one she wore every night since she could walk. I just... I just want to hear her laugh one more time."

Amara's throat constricted. The raw grief in the woman's voice was a physical thing, pressing against her like heat from a forge. She thought of her own grandmother, of all the nights she'd held that blue silk and wondered if she could bear to hear those beloved words again.

"I can't help you," she said gently. "I'm just a seamstress. I mend torn cloth, nothing more."

The woman's expression shifted from pleading to desperate. "I'll pay anything. My husband has gold put aside, jewels from better times. Name your price."

"There is no price because there is no service. I'm sorry for your loss, but—"

"You heartless witch!" The woman's voice cracked like a whip. "My daughter is gone, and you could bring her back, even for a moment, and you refuse? What kind of monster are you?"

"The kind who wants to live," Amara said, beginning to close the door.

The woman shoved against it with surprising strength. "Others will come. Word is spreading through the merchant quarter. They know what you are, what you can do. You can't hide forever."

"Watch me," Amara said, and closed the door firmly. She shot the bolt home and leaned against the rough wood, listening as the woman's footsteps retreated up the stairs.

But the words lingered: *Others will come.*

———◆———

Sleep evaded her. Amara paced the confines of her small room like a caged animal, her mind churning through possibilities. Flee the city? She had no money for travel, no connections beyond Deymar's walls. Hide deeper? There was nowhere in the realm beyond the Guild's reach.

She found herself thinking about the Unraveler—Caedric. Those pale, watchful eyes that had studied her with such uncomfortable intensity. He'd let her go, but she didn't fool herself into thinking he'd lost interest. Men like him were patient hunters, content to wait for their prey to make a mistake.

Why didn't he find proof? The question nagged at her. She'd been able to keep the test fabrics silent during the interrogation, but it had required effort, concentration. If he'd pressed harder, tested her longer...

A chill ran down her spine as understanding dawned. He had found proof—or enough to convince him, at least. He'd released her not because he doubted her guilt, but because he wanted to see what she'd do with her freedom.

She was bait in a trap of his making.

The realization should have terrified her. Instead, it sparked something that felt dangerously like defiance. *If the Guild comes for me again,* she thought, *I won't go quietly.*

Amara moved to her worktable, running her fingers over the familiar tools of her trade. Plain needles, ordinary thread, scraps of fabric that held no memories save what she chose to stitch into them. Simple things, but in her hands, they became something more.

The Guild feared that power, coveted it, would kill to possess it. But it was hers, had always been hers, and she was tired of hiding from—

Her thoughts shattered as her fingers encountered something that didn't belong. A scrap of cloth, no larger than her palm, dark with old stains and rough from long use. She didn't remember placing it there, would never have chosen to keep such a ragged, ugly thing.

The moment she touched it, whispers rose from the weave like smoke from burning hair.

"We are coming for you."

Amara jerked her hand back as if the cloth had burned her. The scrap lay innocent on her table, just another piece of fabric among dozens. But the voice echoed in her memory—cold, hungry, utterly without mercy.

Not the Guild. Something else. Something that made the Unravelers look like gentle shepherds by comparison.

She backed away from the table, her breath coming in short, sharp gasps. Someone had been in her room. Someone had left this message, this warning, this threat.

The Wraithstitchers. It had to be. The cultists who used barbed needles to tear souls from cloth, who wove garments from the essence of the dead. She'd heard whispers of them in the darkest corners of the market, stories told to frighten children and rogue weavers alike.

But why would they want her? What could she possibly—

The answer hit her like a physical blow. Her gift. The ability to bind souls without rune-thread, to awaken memory with nothing but skill and will. In their hands, such power could be turned to darker purposes than comfort or remembrance.

Amara stared at the scrap of cloth, understanding that her world had shifted again. The Guild hunted her for breaking their laws. Desperate mourners would hound her for miracles she couldn't safely provide. And now something far worse stalked her through the shadows, drawn by abilities she'd never asked for and could never fully escape.

She was no longer just hiding from her gift. She was hiding for her life.

Outside her single window, the city settled into uneasy sleep. But Amara remained awake, watching the darkness and wondering what other hunters moved through the night, following the scent of power like wolves following blood.

We are coming for you.

CHAPTER 4
Caedric

The Guild Hall's chamber of records felt like a tomb at this hour, all shadows and silence broken only by the scratch of Caedric's quill against parchment. He'd written dozens of reports over the years, each one a careful balance of facts observed and conclusions drawn. But this one resisted completion, the words seeming to twist under his pen.

Subject: Amara Souster, seamstress, age approximately twenty-five years.

Incident: Multiple witnesses reported auditory manifestations during fabric repair at Lower Market stall. Consistent accounts describe a male voice issuing military commands, attributed to one Captain Thorne (deceased).

Investigation: Subject questioned under standard protocols. No evidence of rune-

thread possession. No reaction to test materials. No admission of unlicensed weaving practices.

Caedric paused, his quill hovering over the parchment. The next line would determine whether the file remained open or closed, whether Amara continued to exist in the Guild's attention or faded back into the anonymity of the common folk.

Conclusion: No proof of unlicensed weaving.

His hand trembled slightly as he wrote the words. Every instinct screamed against them, every year of training and experience insisted he was making a mistake. But the Guild demanded evidence, not instinct. Proof, not suspicion.

He signed his name with sharp, decisive strokes, then set down the quill and stared at the document. Within hours, it would be filed away in the great archives beneath the Guild Hall, joining thousands of similar reports in the vast machinery of bureaucratic oversight.

A soft knock interrupted his brooding. "Enter," he called, though he already knew who it would be.

Needlewarden Korren stepped into the chamber, the rustling sound of his silver-threaded robes reminding Caedric of leaves. The man's face bore the angular severity of someone who'd spent decades enforcing Guild law, and his eyes missed nothing as they fixed on Caedric's report.

"Finished?" Korren asked.

"Yes, sir." Caedric slid the parchment across the table.

Korren read in silence, his expression growing more skeptical with each line. When he reached the conclusion, his eyebrows rose fractionally. "No proof?"

"None that would stand before a tribunal, sir."

"Yet dozens of witnesses heard a dead man's voice rise from the cloth she was mending."

"Fear and suggestion, sir. The power of collective belief to manifest what isn't there."

"Do you believe that, Unraveler?"

The question hung in the air like a blade waiting to fall. Caedric met his superior's gaze steadily. "I believe in evidence, sir. Not rumors."

Korren smiled thinly. "How admirably principled. Tell me, have you heard the reports from the other kingdoms? Sightings of rogue weavers in Valenhall. Phantom armies marching across the borderlands of Theros. The dead walking in the halls of Castle Grimhold."

"I had not, sir."

"The realm grows restless, Caedric. Old magics stir in forgotten corners, and common folk whisper of signs and portents. In such times, even false alarms can spark true fires." Korren set the report down with deliberate care. "Your seamstress may be innocent of weaving, but she is guilty of something far more dangerous—creating hope in the desperate and fear in the faithful."

"What would you have me do, sir?"

"Watch her. Even innocents can become catalysts when the world grows hungry for miracles. And if you are wrong about her abilities, if you have allowed a true rogue to slip through our fingers, you will answer for that failure personally."

"Understood, sir."

"I hope so." Korren moved toward the door, then paused. "Be careful, Unraveler. Sometimes the hunt changes the hunter more than the hunted."

———◆———

Evening had painted the streets of Deymar in shades of amber and shadow by the time Caedric took his position across from Amara's lodgings. He'd changed from his formal black cloak into the unremarkable browns and grays of a common laborer, though he kept his thread-cutter hidden beneath his coat. Observation required invisibility, and the Hemlock Circle's colors were too well known for proper surveillance.

From his vantage point in a doorway, he watched Amara emerge from the tailor's shop above her basement room. She moved with the careful awareness of someone who knew she was being watched, her eyes scanning the street without seeming to do so. But she gave no sign of spotting him.

She stopped at a baker's stall, exchanging coins for a small loaf of bread and a few words with the proprietor. The baker's wife smiled and nodded, treating her like any other customer, but Caedric noticed the subtle distance others maintained. Word of the market incident had spread, creating an invisible barrier around her.

Next came the fishmonger's stall, where she purchased a small piece of cod wrapped in brown paper. Then the herb seller, for what looked like medicinal tea. Simple transactions, the daily routine of someone making a modest living from honest work.

Yet Caedric found himself studying every gesture, every pause, every glance. The way her fingers brushed the fabric of the merchant's awnings as she passed. The careful distance she maintained from anything that might hold strong memories— a veteran's coat, a child's abandoned doll, a woman's mourning veil.

She was being cautious. Too cautious for someone with nothing to hide.

When she turned toward home, Caedric followed at a discrete distance, keeping to the shadows and using the evening crowd for cover. He'd trailed dozens of suspects over the years, learned to read the subtle signs of guilt and innocence in how people moved through the world.

Amara showed neither. Or both. Her composure was perfect, her routine mundane, her behavior utterly ordinary save for that underlying tension that suggested she was performing normalcy rather than living it.

The thought made him angry, though he couldn't say why. Perhaps because she was making him question his own judgment. Or perhaps because she did it with such apparent ease, as if fooling Guild enforcers was just another skill in her repertoire.

She disappeared into the narrow stairway that led to her basement room, and Caedric settled in to wait. Hours of watching had taught him patience, though tonight it felt more like a burden than a virtue.

It was near full dark when he noticed the other observer.

The figure lurked in the shadow of a butcher's shop two streets over, little more than a dark shape against darker stone. But something about the way it held itself—utterly still, unnaturally patient—set

Caedric's nerves on edge. This wasn't a casual passerby or curious neighbor.

Someone else was watching Amara.

Caedric eased from his doorway, moving with the practiced silence of a predator closing on prey. But as he approached the figure's position, it melted away into the network of alleys and side streets that veined the old quarter. He caught a glimpse of dark cloth—not Guild black, but something rougher, stained with substances he didn't want to identify.

When he reached the spot where the watcher had been standing, he found only empty air and the lingering scent of something that made his stomach turn. Old blood, perhaps. Or decay.

Wraithstitchers.

The realization hit him like a physical blow. The cultists had somehow learned of Amara's abilities, or suspected them, and sent their own watchers to evaluate her worth. Which meant she was in more danger than she could imagine.

He thought of Korren's warning about false alarms sparking true fires. If the

Wraithstitchers took Amara, if they somehow confirmed she possessed the abilities he suspected, the consequences would ripple far beyond one seamstress in one market stall.

Caedric hurried back to his post, but the narrow street remained quiet. No sign of Amara, no hint of other watchers. Just shadows and silence and the uncomfortable knowledge that the game had suddenly become far more complex.

———◆———

His quarters in the Guild Hall were sparsely furnished—a narrow bed, a writing desk, and a chest for his few possessions. The walls were bare stone, unadorned save for the crossed thread-cutters that marked his rank within the Hemlock Circle. It was a monk's cell, really, suited to a life of duty and discipline.

Tonight, it felt like a prison.

Caedric sat at his desk, staring at a blank piece of parchment by candlelight. He should be writing a supplemental report about the unknown observer, should be requesting additional resources to investigate possible Wraithstitcher activity in the city.

Instead, he found himself thinking about gold-flecked eyes and the way Amara had held herself during the interrogation—composed, defiant, utterly unbroken despite the weight of Guild authority bearing down on her.

She is a threat, he reminded himself. *A potential rogue weaver whose abilities could destabilize the kingdom's careful balance of power.*

But his mind conjured other images: the careful way she'd folded Captain Thorne's cloak, the respectful manner in which she'd approached the grieving soldier, the quiet dignity with which she'd endured hours of questioning without once losing her composure.

She is Guild business. Nothing more.

The words felt hollow even as he thought them. When had duty become so complicated? When had the simple act of hunting rogues become tangled with unwelcome attraction and grudging respect?

He tried to focus on the facts: unlicensed weaving was forbidden, those who practiced it posed a danger to Guild authority, and his job was to identify and eliminate such threats. Clear, clean, uncomplicated.

But Amara Souster refused to fit into simple categories. She was dangerous, yes—he was certain of that now. But dangerous like a wildfire, or dangerous like a weapon in the wrong hands? The distinction mattered more than he wanted to admit.

Caedric reached for his quill, then stopped. In the candlelight, his hand cast strange shadows on the wall, shapes that reminded him of reaching fingers or grasping claws. Or the delicate movements of someone working a needle through fabric, binding memory into form.

"Amara," he whispered, her name escaping before he could stop it.

The sound hung in the air like an accusation, and Caedric closed his eyes in frustration. This was exactly what Korren had warned him about—the hunt changing the hunter. He was supposed to be above such complications, trained to see past personal feelings to the cold requirements of duty.

But tonight, alone in his room with shadows dancing on the walls, duty felt like a chain around his neck.

Outside his window, the city slept under a blanket of stars. Somewhere in those twisting streets, a seamstress lay in her narrow bed, perhaps dreaming of the whispers that lived in cloth. And somewhere else, darker watchers planned their next move in a game whose stakes neither player fully understood.

Caedric blew out the candle and tried to sleep, but her name echoed in the darkness like a prayer or a curse, and he couldn't decide which frightened him more.

CHAPTER 5
Amara

The morning sun slanted across the market, but Amara's stall remained untouched by its warmth. She sat behind her workbench, hands folded in her lap, watching the familiar dance of commerce flow around her like water around a stone. Merchants called their wares, children darted between cart wheels, and life continued its eternal rhythm—but she might as well have been invisible.

Her regular customers found urgent business elsewhere. The cobbler who usually brought her his difficult repairs now hurried past without meeting her eyes. The baker's wife, who once stopped to share gossip and small coins for mending tears, crossed to the opposite side of the street entirely.

But others lingered. They gathered at the edges of her vision like moths drawn to flame, whispering among themselves while stealing glances at her stall. A woman in a merchant's coat clutched what looked like a child's shoe. An old man held a bundle wrapped in oilcloth, his eyes fixed on Amara's hands. A young soldier—barely more than a boy—fingered the torn sleeve of his uniform with desperate hope.

They wanted what she couldn't give.

"Seamstress." The woman with the child's shoe stepped forward, her voice carefully controlled. "I heard... that is, people say you can make cloth remember things."

"I mend tears and replace buttons," Amara replied without looking up from the scrap of fabric she'd been pretending to examine. "Nothing more."

"My son's shoe. He... he died last winter. The fever." The woman's composure cracked slightly. "But he loved these shoes, wore them everywhere. If you could just—"

"I'm sorry for your loss." Amara finally met the woman's eyes, seeing the familiar weight of grief there. "But I can't help you the way you hope."

"Can't, or won't?"

The question hung in the air between them. Amara felt the weight of other stares, the hungry attention of those who believed miracles could be purchased like bolts of cloth.

"Both," she said quietly.

The woman's face hardened. "My gold isn't good enough for your magic?" she spat, loud enough for others to hear.

"There is no magic."

"Then explain what happened with the soldier's cloak. Explain why half the market heard a dead man's voice."

Amara had no answer that wouldn't damn her further. The woman waited a moment longer, then turned away with a disgusted sound. But others took her place—a steady stream of desperate souls clutching remnants of the dead, each one convinced that whispered rumors held more truth than careful denials.

By midday, Amara's coin purse remained as light as it had been at dawn, but her heart felt heavy as lead. Each rejected plea added weight to the growing certainty that her quiet life was truly over.

The walk home felt longer than usual, every shadow potentially hiding watchers. Amara kept her pace steady, her expression neutral, but inside her thoughts churned like storm-tossed water.

Her basement room welcomed her with familiar gloom, unchanged despite the upheaval in her life. She lit the oil lamp and settled at her small table, pulling out the piece of faded blue fabric she'd stitched over the night before. She sliced the new threads and ran her fingers over the material.

"Cloth remembers, little one," her grandmother had said, so many years ago it felt like a dream. *"But not everyone can hear what it has to say."*

Eight-year-old Amara had thought it was just another of Grandmother's stories, like the tales of fairy queens who lived in flower petals or dragons that nested in clouds. She'd been helping with the mending that day, learning to make neat, small stitches while her grandmother worked on a complicated quilt.

"Listen," the old woman had whispered, her needle moving through the patchwork with practiced ease. *"Do you hear it?"*

And Amara had listened, pressing her ear close to the fabric, until she heard what might have been laughter—children's voices, bright with joy, woven into the very threads. At the time, she'd thought it was her imagination, or perhaps the wind through the window making the cloth rustle.

Now, she knew better.

Her grandmother had possessed the same gift, the same curse. Had hidden it just as carefully, used it just as sparingly. But she'd been luckier—the Guild's grip had been looser then, their paranoia less consuming. Or perhaps she'd simply been more skilled at keeping secrets.

Amara touched the blue silk gently, feeling the echo of familiar hands, the whisper of half-remembered lullabies. Her grandmother's voice lived in this scrap, patient and loving, waiting for the right stitch to set it free.

But awakening it would serve no purpose except her own comfort, and comfort was a luxury she could no longer afford.

Instead, she pulled out other scraps from her collection—pieces she'd gathered over the years, some found, some brought by customers, all heavy with the weight of memory. A bloodstained kerchief that whispered of a duel gone wrong. A child's mitten that held the echo of snowball fights and winter laughter. A soldier's sash that reeked of smoke and rang with the clash of steel.

Each piece called to her, begging to be awakened, to have its stories told one more time. But Amara had a different purpose for them.

She threaded her plainest needle with ordinary cotton and began to stitch—again, not to wake, but to silence. Each piece required a different approach: the kerchief needed tight, binding stitches that wrapped the memories like bandages around a wound. The mitten responded to gentle persuasion, its cheerful whispers fading to murmurs under her careful attention. The soldier's sash fought her, its violent memories clawing at her concentration until sweat beaded on her forehead.

With each success, the voices grew quieter. But the effort left her drained, her hands shaking with exhaustion. When she tried to set down the needle, her fingers cramped around it, reluctant to release the tool that had become an extension of her will.

Blood welled from tiny punctures she didn't remember making, the telltale mark of threadburn—again. Each drop was a payment extracted by her gift, a reminder that power always came with a price.

This is what control costs, she thought, wrapping her bleeding fingertips in clean cloth. *Not just the effort, but pieces of myself.*

Still, it was possible. She could silence the whispers if she had to, could press the memories back into dormancy. It wouldn't make her normal—nothing could do that—but it might help her hide.

If hiding was even still an option.

A sharp knock at her door shattered the evening quiet. Amara froze, her heart hammering against her ribs. The Guild? Or perhaps one of the desperate souls from the market, unwilling to accept her refusal?

The knock came again, more insistent but not aggressive. A man's voice called through the wood: "Seamstress? I mean no harm. I just need to speak with you."

She recognized the voice—Sigmund, a wool merchant who occasionally brought her garments for repair. A steady customer, always polite, never troublesome. What could he want at this hour?

Against her better judgment, she cracked the door open. Sigmund stood in the narrow stairwell, his usual merchant's confidence replaced by nervous energy. His eyes darted over her shoulder, as if checking for eavesdroppers.

"May I come in? What I have to say isn't for the street."

She considered refusing, but curiosity won over caution. Sigmund had never shown interest in anything beyond honest business. Perhaps he simply wanted to warn her about the market gossip.

She stepped aside, and he entered quickly, closing the door behind him.

"Did you truly awaken a dead man's voice?" The question was direct, almost brutal in its simplicity.

"No," Amara lied smoothly. "People heard what they wanted to hear."

Sigmund studied her face in the lamplight, then nodded slowly. "Perhaps. Or perhaps you're wiser than you appear." He moved to her single window, peering up at the street through the glass. "Either way, you should know—the Guild may not be your only concern."

"What do you mean?"

"I have... connections in the merchant quarter. Men who trade in information rather than silk and spices." His voice dropped to barely above a whisper. "Word is spreading about your incident. There are those who seek weavers with unusual gifts. Not to prosecute them, but to use them."

The Wraithstitchers. He didn't need to name them for Amara to understand.

"I've done nothing to attract such attention."

"Haven't you?" Sigmund's smile held no warmth. "A seamstress who can wake the dead would be valuable indeed to certain... collectors. Whether you meant to display such abilities or not."

He turned from the window, his expression serious. "If I were you, I'd leave Deymar before the Hemlock Circle decides to take another look at your case. Or before worse than the Guild comes knocking."

After he left, Amara sat in the gathering darkness, considering his words. Flee the city, abandon everything she'd built, start over somewhere else with nothing but her needles and the dangerous secret she carried in her hands.

It would be the sensible choice. The safe choice.

But as she looked around her small room—at the worktable where she'd learned to master her gift, at the chest that held her grandmother's memory, at the familiar walls that had sheltered her for so many years—she felt something harden inside her chest.

She was tired of hiding. Tired of denying what she was, of pretending her gift was a curse rather than a heritage passed down through generations. Tired of letting fear dictate her choices.

Amara pulled her workbasket closer, selecting threads with deliberate care. If the

Guild wanted to hunt her, if the Wraithstitchers sought to claim her, if the desperate masses demanded miracles she couldn't provide—let them all come.

She threaded her needle with steady hands, her grandmother's lessons echoing in her memory. *Cloth remembers, little one. But not everyone can hear what it has to say.*

"If they come for me again," she whispered to the dancing lamplight, "they'll find I am not so helpless."

Outside her window, the city settled into uneasy sleep. But Amara remained awake, practicing her stitches by lamplight, each one a small act of defiance against those who would control or destroy her.

She would not run. Not anymore.

Let the hunters come. They would discover what it meant to pursue a seamstress who could bind more than thread—one who could weave the very essence of memory into weapons of her own making.

CHAPTER 6
Caedric

The Guild Hall's highest tower cast a shadow like a sword across the courtyard, and Caedric felt its weight as he climbed the spiraling stone steps. Each footfall echoed in the narrow stairwell, a metronome marking his approach toward what he suspected would be an unpleasant conversation.

The chamber at the tower's peak served as the domain of Needlewarden Thessa, one of the few women to reach such heights within the Guild hierarchy. Her silver-threaded robes caught the morning light streaming through tall windows, and her pale eyes—so like his own—fixed on him with predatory intensity.

"Sit," she commanded without preamble.

Caedric took the chair across from her desk, noting the way her fingers drummed against the polished wood. In seven years of service, he'd learned to read the Guild's moods through such small tells. Thessa was angry, though her expression remained perfectly controlled.

"You released her," she said. Not a question.

"I found no evidence of unlicensed weaving, as Guild law requires—"

"Guild law." Her voice cut through his explanation like a blade through silk. "Tell me, Unraveler, what good is law when it allows threats to slip through our fingers?"

"With respect, ma'am, we cannot simply imprison citizens based on rumors and fear."

Thessa leaned forward, her eyes glittering with cold light. "Cannot? Or will not?" She pulled a leather folder from her desk drawer, spreading its contents before him. "Three reports in the past week alone. A merchant's daughter in Valenhall claims she can weave prophecy into silk. A shepherd boy near the Theros border speaks of hearing his dead father's voice in a woolen cloak. An old woman in Castle Grimhold's lower city has been selling 'memory quilts' that supposedly hold the essence of the departed."

Caedric studied the reports, recognizing the careful bureaucratic language that transformed human desperation into neat administrative categories. "Unsubstantiated claims—"

"Are becoming substantiated actions." Thessa's finger stabbed at one particular document. "A merchant's daughter was found dead yesterday, her throat cut with what appears to be a barbed needle. Sound familiar?"

The Wraithstitchers. Caedric's blood chilled, though he kept his expression neutral. "You believe the cultists are involved?"

"I believe the realm grows hungry for miracles, and miracles attract those who would devour them." She gathered the reports with sharp, efficient movements. "Your seamstress may have convinced you of her innocence, but she has not convinced the desperate souls flocking to her market stall. Nor has she convinced whoever was watching her across from her lodgings."

"Someone is watching her?" he asked, feigning ignorance.

"As you should have been doing." The rebuke struck like a physical blow. "Instead, you filed a report declaring her harmless and walked away. Do you have any idea what failure to control rogue weavers does to the Guild's authority in a city like Deymar?"

Caedric forced himself to meet her gaze. "It undermines public confidence in our oversight."

"It does more than that. It creates the impression that unauthorized magic is tolerable, even safe. And that impression spreads like plague through frightened populations." Thessa stood, moving to the window that overlooked the city. "The Guild's power rests on a simple principle: we alone determine who may touch the threads of memory. The moment common folk believe otherwise..."

"The monopoly crumbles," Caedric finished.

"Precisely." She turned back to him, her expression harder than before. "Which brings me to your new assignment."

The orders came written on Guild parchment, sealed with silver thread that would dissolve if opened by unauthorized hands. Caedric broke the seal in the privacy of his quarters, scanning the formal language that masked urgent concern.

Report of Disturbance: Three leagues northeast of Deymar, abandoned Kellner farmstead. Patrol Unit Seven reported auditory anomalies and evidence of textile manipulation. Investigate immediately. Detain any individuals found on premises.

Below the official text, a note in Thessa's precise handwriting: *The wolves are circling, Unraveler. Determine which kind before they bite.*

Within the hour, Caedric rode out with two other Hemlock enforcers: Jorik, a grizzled veteran whose thread-cutter bore notches marking successful captures, and Kess, a younger man whose enthusiasm for the hunt made up for his lack of experience. Neither spoke much as they followed the winding road away from Deymar's walls, but Caedric sensed their tension.

Reports of "textile manipulation" usually meant one of two things: either a rogue weaver had lost control of their abilities, or the Wraithstitchers had claimed another victim. Either way, the scene rarely left witnesses in a condition to provide testimony.

The Kellner farmstead had been abandoned for years, its fields gone to weeds and its buildings slowly surrendering to time and weather. But as they approached the main house, Caedric knew immediately that something terrible had happened here.

The walls were scarred with threadlike patterns—not carved or painted, but *woven* into the stone itself. Silver lines traced impossible geometries across the weathered surface, pulsing with a faint, sickly light that hurt to look at directly. Around the foundation, scraps of fabric lay scattered like fallen leaves: torn shirts, shredded dresses, the remains of a child's blanket that still held faint stains of blood.

"Gods preserve us," Kess whispered, dismounting with visible reluctance.

Caedric drew his thread-cutter, feeling comfort in its familiar weight in his hand. The silver blade hummed with contained energy, designed to cut through any weaving—authorized or otherwise. But as he approached the scarred walls, he wondered if it would be enough.

"Jorik, circle around back. Kess, check the outbuildings. Shout if you find anything." His voice carried more confidence than he felt.

The patterns on the walls weren't random—they followed a logic that made his eyes water and his stomach lurch. This was unraveling magic, the forbidden art that the Wraithstitchers practiced in their hidden sanctuaries. Not content to merely weave memory into fabric, they tore souls apart thread by thread, using the raw material to craft garments of terrible power.

Inside the farmhouse, the devastation was complete. Furniture lay overturned, windows shattered, and in the center of what had once been a kitchen, a circular pattern was burned into the floorboards. Around it, more fabric scraps, these ones still whispering with the voices of the dead—but not comfortable, loving whispers like those Amara might awaken. These were screams, compressed into cloth, the dying agonies of souls torn apart by barbed needles.

Caedric knelt beside one particular scrap—a woman's shawl that might once have been blue. When he touched it with the tip of his thread-cutter, it dissolved instantly, the silver blade cutting through the malevolent weaving that held it together. But not before he heard the echo of a voice, wordless with pain.

"Sir!" Kess's shout came from outside. "You need to see this!"

Behind the farmhouse, in what had once been a vegetable garden, Kess stood beside a makeshift altar built from broken furniture and twisted metal. Draped across it were more garments, but these were different— whole, untorn, arranged with ritualistic precision.

"They were practicing," Caedric realized, studying the scene. "Using the other victims to power their work, and these..." He gestured at the altar. "These were the successes."

Each garment glowed with that same sickly light as the wall patterns, but the radiance was more controlled, more purposeful. A cloak that whispered strategies in a dozen different voices. A pair of gloves that flexed with phantom hands. A dress that seemed to move as if worn by an invisible woman.

This was what the Wraithstitchers created when they had enough raw material to work with—not just echoes of the dead, but weapons.

"Burn it all," Caedric commanded. "Every scrap, every thread. Nothing leaves this place."

As his men worked to build a pyre, Caedric found himself thinking of Amara. Could her gift accomplish what these cultists achieved only through torture and murder? If so, she would be invaluable to them. And completely helpless against their methods.

The ride back to Deymar passed in contemplative silence, the smoke from their pyre a black smudge against the afternoon sky. Jorik and Kess peeled off toward the Guild Hall to file their report, but Caedric found himself taking a different path through the city streets.

He needed to think, needed to reconcile what he'd seen with what he believed about duty and justice and the complicated woman who had somehow become the center of his professional attention.

The Kellner farmstead had been butchered by monsters wearing human faces. They killed not for survival or even profit, but for the raw pleasure of unmade souls writhing in their hands. Against such creatures, Guild protocols seemed suddenly inadequate—not wrong, perhaps, but insufficient.

If the Wraithstitchers find her first...

The thought lodged in his mind like a splinter. Amara might be guilty of unlicensed weaving, might be a threat to Guild authority, might be everything Thessa claimed she was. But she didn't deserve to end up as raw material for the cultists' next atrocity.

As evening descended on the city, Caedric stationed himself in the familiar doorway across from her lodgings. Through the small window of her basement room, he could see lamplight flickering as she moved about her evening routine. So normal, so mundane—yet he knew now that normal was an illusion, a thin veneer painted over the world.

His thoughts warred with themselves as he watched her silhouette pass back and forth behind the glass. Every principle of his training demanded that he arrest her, drag her before a Guild tribunal, force her to confess the abilities she possessed. But something deeper, something that spoke in his own voice rather than Thessa's, whispered a different truth.

She was caught between forces larger than herself—Guild suspicion on one side, cult hunger on the other. And while he couldn't yet determine her guilt or innocence, he could ensure that whichever verdict emerged, it would be delivered by proper authority rather than barbed needles in the dark.

As an Unraveler, I should drag her to the Guild before it's too late, he told himself. *As a man, I cannot ignore that she's caught in something she doesn't deserve.*

The conflict between duty and instinct should have been resolved by his training, by years of conditioning that placed Guild law above personal feeling. But the afternoon's discoveries had shifted something fundamental in his worldview. The Guild hunted rogues to maintain order—but the Wraithstitchers hunted them to feed chaos.

In such a world, which was the greater evil?

Caedric settled deeper into the shadows, his thread-cutter within easy reach but somehow less comforting than usual. Whatever Amara was—innocent seamstress or dangerous rogue—he would watch over her until the truth revealed itself.

And if the Wraithstitchers came for her before that truth emerged, they would find that she had acquired an unexpected guardian.

One who had seen what they did to their victims, and who would die before allowing such horrors to claim another soul.

CHAPTER 7
Amara

The market felt different now, as if Amara moved through a world that might collapse at the wrong word or gesture. Conversations died when she approached, only to resume in urgent whispers once she'd passed. Children pointed and tugged at their mothers' skirts, while the adults whispered, "thread-witch."

She arranged her tools with deliberate calm, threading needles and sorting fabric scraps as if normalcy could be imposed through routine. But her customers came in a thin trickle—a torn hem here, a loose button there—and even those brave enough to approach her stall maintained careful distance, as if the gift she might possess could contaminate them through proximity.

At least she had some work, even if it wasn't much.

The morning sun climbed higher, and with it, the weight of watching eyes. Amara felt them from every direction: merchants pretending to arrange their wares while stealing glances, housewives clustering in doorways to whisper behind their hands, even the city guards seeming more attentive than usual as they made their rounds.

But it was the sound of iron-shod wheels on cobblestone that made her truly nervous.

The carriage that rolled into the market was an intrusion of wealth into a world of copper coins and haggled prices. Black lacquered wood gleamed with silver fittings, and the horses that pulled it were bred for beauty as much as strength. Conversations didn't just die at its approach—they fled, leaving an uncomfortable silence in their wake.

When the carriage door opened and a woman emerged, Amara understood why. Lady Selanna Veyra moved with the fluid grace of nobility, her mourning dress of finest silk making every other garment in the market look crude by comparison. A black veil covered her face, but it couldn't hide the way her shoulders held themselves—rigid with grief barely contained.

She approached Amara's stall with deliberate steps, each one echoing against the sudden quiet. Around them, the market held its breath.

"You are the seamstress," Lady Selanna said. Her voice carried the cultured tones of court education, but underneath lay something raw and desperate. "The one they speak of."

"I mend clothing, my lady. Nothing more."

"Nothing more?" Selanna lifted her veil, revealing a face that might once have been beautiful but was now carved hollow by loss. Her eyes held the emptiness that came from outliving one's children. "Then explain why my servants whisper your name in the same breath as 'miracle' and 'forbidden magic.'"

Amara forced herself to meet that devastated gaze. "Servants whisper many things, my lady. Few of them true."

"My son is dead." The words fell like stones into still water. "Drowned in the river three weeks past, trying to save a merchant's cart horse that had broken through the ice.

Seventeen years old, and he died for a stranger's beast because that was the kind of boy he was."

The pain in her voice was a physical thing, pressing against Amara like heat from a forge. She'd heard such grief before, in the voices of those who brought her scraps and fragments, begging for one last word from the departed. But coming from nobility, it carried additional weight.

"I'm sorry for your loss," Amara said carefully.

"Are you?" Selanna reached into her reticule and withdrew a bundle of blue silk—a young man's tunic, embroidered with the wolf's head of House Veyra. "This was his favorite. He wore it to festivals, to court functions, even to go riding when he should have worn something more practical." Her fingers traced the silver thread with reverence. "It still smells like him. Still holds the shape of his shoulders."

The tunic whispered to Amara even from a distance. Not words, but something deeper— the echo of laughter, the warmth of young flesh, the mixture of pride and affection that came from being someone's beloved son. It would be so easy to awaken those memories, to let the boy's voice speak one more time through fabric that had known his touch.

It would also be utterly catastrophic.

"My lady, I understand your pain, but—"

"Do you?" Selanna's voice sharpened like a blade being drawn. "Do you understand what it means to bury your only child? To know that your bloodline ends with you, that everything you've built will crumble into dust because there's no one left to carry it forward?"

"I'm sorry. I cannot help you."

"I have gold, seamstress. More gold than you'll see in ten years of mending torn hems. I have connections at court, influence with the merchant guilds, protection from those who might... wish you harm."

The offer was tempting in ways that had nothing to do with wealth. Protection from the Guild, from the whispered threats, from the growing sense that forces beyond her understanding were circling like wolves. All for one stitch, one careful awakening of memories already straining to be free.

"I'm just a seamstress," Amara repeated, but the words felt hollow.

Selanna's expression hardened. "Don't lie to me, girl. I've heard the stories. I've spoken to witnesses. That soldier's cloak sang with the captain's voice, and you were the one holding the needle." She leaned forward, her voice dropping to a whisper that somehow carried more menace than any shout. "If you won't help me willingly, I'm sure I can find ways to make you."

The threat was delicately delivered but unmistakable. Refuse, and Lady Selanna would ensure that Amara's troubles multiplied exponentially. Accept, and... what? Word would spread that the seamstress could indeed wake the dead, drawing every desperate soul in the kingdom to her door.

"I... I need time to consider," Amara said finally.

"Time is a luxury I don't possess." But Selanna stepped back, her business manner reasserting itself over raw grief. "I'll return tomorrow for your answer. Choose wisely, seamstress. There are worse things than noble patronage in this world."

She swept back to her carriage with the same fluid grace, leaving behind only the lingering scent of expensive perfume.

As the carriage rolled away, Amara became aware of the market slowly returning to life around her. Conversations resumed, but at lower volumes, and she caught fragments that made her blood run cold: "...House Veyra... powerful family... what did she want with..."

But it was another presence that truly unsettled her. Across the square, half-hidden in the shadow of a bakery's awning, Caedric watched. Their eyes met for a heartbeat, and in that moment, she saw something that hadn't been there during his interrogation—not just the cold assessment of a hunter, but something almost like concern.

Had he heard Lady Selanna's offer? Her threats? If so, what would he make of them?

His pale gaze held hers for another moment, then he melted back into the crowd. But the feeling of being watched remained, pressing against her.

⁕

As Amara walked home, her mind churned through possibilities, each one worse than the last. Refuse Lady Selanna, and face the wrath of House Veyra plus whatever additional attention the noblewoman might draw to her situation. Accept, and confirm every suspicion the Guild harbored while painting a target on herself for anyone else seeking such services.

The familiar gloom of her basement room welcomed her, but even here she found no peace. The walls felt closer than before, the ceiling lower, as if the very space was contracting around her. She lit her oil lamp and settled at her worktable, staring at the collection of needles and thread that had once represented simple, honest work.

Now they felt like instruments of a fate she'd never chosen.

"We are coming for you."

The whisper from that cursed scrap of cloth echoed in her memory, more urgent now in light of Lady Selanna's visit. The noblewoman represented pressure from above—wealth and influence demanding miracles. But the Wraithstitchers represented something far worse: those who would take her gift by force, tear it from her with barbed needles and leave nothing but an empty shell behind.

Between the Guild's suspicion, the nobles' demands, and the cultists' hunger, she was trapped in a web that tightened with every choice she didn't make.

The sound of her grandmother's voice drifted up from memory: *"Power is never a gift, little one. It's always a burden. The only choice is whether you carry it or let it carry you."*

But her grandmother had lived in simpler times, when the Guild's grip was looser and the shadows held fewer monsters. She'd never faced nobles offering gold with one hand while sharpening knives with the other. She'd never felt the weight of watching eyes from every direction, never known the terror of being hunted by things that wore human faces.

Amara rose from her chair and moved to the single window, peering up at the street through the glass. The evening crowd was thinning, merchants closing their stalls and families returning to warm hearths. Normal life, proceeding as it always had while her own world crumbled at the edges.

A movement in the shadows across the street caught her attention. Not Caedric this time—she'd learned to recognize his particular way of holding himself, the careful stillness that marked his surveillance. This was someone else, a cloaked figure that lingered too long in the doorway of a closed shop before melting away into the maze of alleys beyond.

The Wraithstitchers. She was certain of it now. They'd moved beyond leaving cursed scraps and cryptic warnings. They were watching, waiting, perhaps planning their approach.

Amara stepped back from the window, her heart hammering against her ribs. The walls weren't just closing in metaphorically—they were closing in from all sides, cutting off escape routes and forcing her toward choices she wasn't ready to make.

She looked at her worktable, at the tools of her trade and the scraps of fabric that whispered with stored memories. Tomorrow, Lady Selanna would return for her answer.

Tomorrow, the Guild might decide she'd had enough rope to hang herself. Tomorrow, the Wraithstitchers might tire of watching and act.

Outside, the city settled into uneasy darkness while predators of various kinds sharpened their claws and prepared for the hunt to begin in earnest.

CHAPTER 8
Caedric

The Guild Hall's corridors hummed with whispers that died the moment Caedric appeared. He caught fragments as he passed—"seamstress," "market incident," "voices from cloth"—but the archivists and junior clerks fell silent under his gaze, suddenly finding urgent business in their ledgers and filing systems.

The whispers followed him anyway, clinging like smoke to his black cloak. Word of Amara had infected even these sacred halls, spreading through the Guild's careful hierarchy like a contagion that threatened their monopoly on truth.

"Unraveler."

Caedric turned to find Needlewarden Korren approaching with the measured stride of a man carrying bad news.

"Sir."

"Walk with me." It wasn't a request.

They moved through the Hall's deeper chambers, past rooms where novices learned to distinguish between authorized and forbidden weaving, past the locked vaults that held confiscated relics. The silence stretched between them until Korren finally spoke.

"The seamstress grows troublesome."

"She remains under observation, sir."

"Does she?" Korren stopped beside a window that overlooked the city. In the distance, smoke rose from the market district—cooking fires, forge smoke, the ordinary business of life continuing while shadows gathered at its edges. "Because my informants tell me that Lady Selanna Veyra paid her a visit yesterday. A very public visit, in a very fine carriage, with a very specific request."

Caedric kept his expression neutral, though inwardly he cursed. The Guild's network of informants reached into every corner of Deymar, including places he'd thought beyond their immediate attention.

"I observed the meeting, sir. The seamstress refused whatever service the Lady requested."

"Ah." Korren's pale eyes glittered with cold light. "So, she does provide services. Interesting how that detail was absent from your report."

The trap closed around him with elegant precision. Either Amara was guilty of unlicensed weaving, or she was guilty of fraud—claiming abilities she didn't possess to extract payment from grieving nobles. In the Guild's logic, both crimes demanded the same solution.

"The Circle's reputation depends on certainty, Caedric. Not observation, not speculation—certainty. If she is guilty, you must prove it. If she is innocent, you must prove that as well. No more half-measures."

"And if the proof is... inconclusive, sir?"

Korren smiled. "Then we must make it conclusive. Every rumor of unauthorized weaving feeds the flames of chaos. Better one seamstress suffer than the entire kingdom fall to rogue magic."

The dismissal was clear. Caedric bowed stiffly and retreated, but the conversation's implications followed him like ravenous shadows. The Guild wanted a conclusion—guilty or innocent mattered less than having an official verdict to present to the world.

<hr />

House Veyra occupied a hill overlooking Deymar's merchant quarter, its ancient walls bearing the scars of centuries. Black banners hung from every tower, mourning cloth draped the windows, and the very air seemed heavy with loss.

Caedric approached the main gates under the pretense of investigating Wraithstitcher activity—not entirely a lie, given what he'd observed at the Kellner farmstead. The guards recognized his black cloak and silver thread-cutter, waving him through with nervous deference.

Inside, the manor felt like a tomb. Servants moved with muffled steps, their voices barely above whispers. The halls that had once echoed with laughter now absorbed sound like black cloth absorbed light, creating a suffocating atmosphere of controlled despair.

Lady Selanna received him in her private chambers. She sat beside a cold fireplace, still veiled, her hands folded over what looked like a piece of blue fabric.

"Unraveler." Her voice carried the hollow courtesy of nobility forced to acknowledge authority they couldn't buy or influence. "To what do I owe this visit?"

"I'm investigating reports of unusual magical activity in the city. Your name came up in connection with a certain seamstress."

Something shifted in her posture—tension, perhaps, or calculation. "I sought her services, yes. A mother's grief makes one... susceptible to hope."

"What services did you request?"

The question hung between them. Selanna's fingers tightened on the blue fabric, and for a moment her composure cracked, revealing the raw wound beneath.

"I asked her to bring my son's voice back. To let me hear him laugh one more time." The words came out as broken whispers. "She refused."

"Did she give a reason?"

"She claimed to be nothing more than a seamstress. A lie, of course—half the city heard a voice rise from the cloak when she mended it. But she wouldn't help me. Wouldn't even try."

Caedric studied her carefully, noting the way grief and manipulation warred in her voice. She was broken, yes, but not helpless. The kind of dangerous combination that turned mourning mothers into weapons against those who denied them comfort.

"May I see the garment?"

Selanna hesitated, then unfolded the blue silk. It was a young man's tunic, finely made, embroidered with silver thread that formed the wolf's head of House Veyra. The moment Caedric looked at it, he felt something—a faint tug at the edges of his consciousness, whispers trying to surface from the fabric's weave.

When he reached toward it, the sensation grew stronger. Not voices, exactly, but the echo of them, as if someone had begun to awaken the memories the silk contained, then stopped halfway through the process.

"Don't touch it," Selanna said sharply, pulling the tunic back. "It's all I have left of him."

But Caedric had felt enough. Someone had worked magic on that fabric—not completed the weaving, but begun it. Started to draw memory from cloth, then abandoned the effort. The question was whether that someone had been Amara or another practitioner entirely.

"I'll need to examine your son's chambers," he said.

"Why?"

"To determine if there are any signs of unauthorized magical activity."

It was Guild authority speaking, and Selanna couldn't refuse without arousing more suspicion. She led him through corridors heavy with mourning cloth to a suite of rooms that had been preserved exactly as their occupant had left them.

The chambers spoke of a young man coming into his own—riding gear mixed with scholarly texts, weapons crossed with musical instruments, the eclectic collection of someone still discovering his place in the world. But what caught Caedric's attention were the subtle signs of disturbance: drawers that had been searched and carefully rearranged, belongings that had been moved and replaced with almost perfect precision.

Someone had been here. Someone looking for fabric that might hold the boy's essence.

As they returned to the main hall, Caedric noted other details that hadn't registered on his initial approach. Threads of unusual color worked into the tapestries. Patterns in the floor mosaics that seemed to shift when observed peripherally. The faint scent of something that made his skin crawl.

Near the outer walls, he found what he was looking for: scraps of fabric caught on rose thorns, their weave torn in specific patterns that had nothing to do with natural snagging. These were deliberate cuts, made by barbed instruments designed to unravel souls from cloth.

The Wraithstitchers had been here. Recently.

"Lady Selanna," he said as they reached the entrance hall, "I must ask—have you noticed any unusual visitors lately? Strangers asking about your son, or showing interest in his belongings?"

Her pause lasted a heartbeat too long. "No. No one of that sort."

The lie was obvious, but Caedric didn't press. Instead, he bowed formally and took his leave, filing away every detail for later consideration. As he walked back toward the city, pieces of a larger puzzle began to arrange themselves in his mind.

Lady Selanna had approached Amara publicly, offering wealth and protection in exchange for forbidden services. When refused, she'd made veiled threats. But privately, she'd already allowed—or perhaps invited—far darker practitioners into her home.

The Wraithstitchers weren't just watching Amara. They were positioning themselves, using grief-stricken nobles as unwitting allies in their hunt for new victims. And if Lady Selanna was involved, willingly or not, then Amara faced threats from directions she couldn't even see.

Back in his sparse quarters, Caedric sat at his desk and stared at a blank piece of parchment. He should be writing a report about House Veyra, documenting evidence of Wraithstitcher activity, requesting additional resources to investigate the connection between noble grief and cult recruitment.

Instead, he found himself thinking about Amara's refusal of Lady Selanna's offer. Most rogue weavers he'd encountered were driven by desperation or ambition, willing to take any risk for the right price.

But Amara had turned down wealth, protection, and noble patronage. Had resisted the temptation to use her abilities even when threatened with Guild retribution. That showed a level of control and principle that most licensed weavers lacked, let alone rogues operating in the shadows.

If she truly possessed the gift—and his every instinct said she did—then she was using it responsibly, carefully, with full awareness of the consequences. The Guild should be recruiting her, not hunting her.

Instead, the Guild suspected her of crimes she'd committed only in the service of compassion. Nobles like Lady Selanna would use her grief as a weapon against her. And the

Wraithstitchers would tear her apart thread by thread if they got the chance.

"What am I missing?" he murmured to the darkening sky.

The answer felt close, tantalizingly near, but it slipped away like smoke whenever he tried to grasp it. There was a pattern here, connections between Guild policy and noble desperation and cult activity that he couldn't quite see. But every instinct honed by seven years of hunting rogues told him that Amara Souster was the key to understanding it all.

And that understanding her might require him to choose between duty and truth—a choice that would define not just her fate, but his own.

CHAPTER 9
Amara

The next morning, the market square felt like a stage where the audience had abandoned her mid-performance. The arrival of a noble had driven away most of her meager clientele, and she sat behind her workbench, hands folded in her lap, watching the crowd.

Is Caedric among them? The thought made her skin crawl. She'd grown accustomed to his form of surveillance, the way he held himself with predatory stillness. But now she couldn't be certain which eyes belonged to the Guild and which to other, darker observers.

She turned her attention back to the simple repair—a coat with a torn seam, honest work that required no gift beyond steady hands. But even that small task felt impossible under the weight of so much scrutiny. Every stitch might be analyzed, every pause interpreted as evidence of forbidden practices. She found herself starting at sudden sounds, her eyes darting toward every movement in her peripheral vision.

This cannot continue, she thought, setting down her needle with hands that shook despite her efforts at control. *I'll go mad from the watching before anyone decides what to do with me.*

As if summoned by her desperation, the sound of iron-shod wheels on cobblestone cut through the market's murmur. The same black carriage as before, its silver fittings catching the sunlight like bared teeth. Conversations died in its wake, leaving a spreading pool of silence that followed its progress toward her stall.

This time, Lady Selanna was not alone.

Four guards in House Veyra's colors flanked the carriage, their hands resting casually on sword hilts. They moved with confidence, and their presence transformed the market from a place of commerce into something that felt dangerously like a trap.

Lady Selanna emerged from the carriage with the same fluid grace as before, but her mourning dress was different. More formal, more ornate, the kind of garment worn to make statements rather than simply observe proprieties. Her veil was black silk that caught the light like a dark gemstone, and beneath it, Amara caught glimpses of a face that held no trace of yesterday's desperate pleading.

This was nobility in its most dangerous aspect: grief hardened into purpose, wealth transformed into weapon.

"Seamstress," Lady Selanna's voice carried clearly across the suddenly quiet square. She approached Amara's stall with deliberate steps, each one echoing against the stone like a countdown. "I've come for your answer."

"My lady, I told you yesterday—"

"You told me you needed time to consider. Time I have given you." Selanna's voice rose, pitched to carry to the watching crowd. "And now I ask again: will you help a grieving mother speak with her dead child?"

Ripples of whispers spread outward from her stall—*dead child, grieving mother, the seamstress who can wake the dead*—while every eye fixed on Amara with renewed intensity.

"I cannot help you, my lady. I am just—"

"Just a seamstress?" Selanna laughed mirthlessly. "The entire market heard Captain Thorne's voice rise from his cloak when you mended it. Are we all mad? Did we all imagine the same impossible thing?"

Amara felt the crowd's mood shift around her like a tide turning. Some faces showed sympathy for the noble lady's grief. Others held accusation—if she possessed such power and refused to use it, what kind of monster was she? A few displayed the hungry calculation of those who saw opportunity in others' desperation.

"Please," Amara said quietly, "lower your voice. There's no need to—"

"Lower my voice?" Selanna stepped closer to the stall, her guards moving to flank her. "Should I whisper my grief? Should I hide my need because it makes others uncomfortable?" Her voice cracked with genuine pain, but underneath lay something harder, more dangerous. "My son is dead, seamstress. And you—you who can bring voices back from cloth—refuse to let me hear his laughter one more time."

The crowd murmured, a sound like distant thunder. Amara caught fragments: *"…heartless…" "…my own child died…" "…if she can help…"* The sympathy was shifting toward Selanna, as it always did when nobility displayed their wounds in public.

"Come with me," Selanna commanded. "My carriage is waiting. We'll go to my home, where you can work in privacy, and I'll pay you more gold than you've seen in your lifetime."

"I cannot—"

"If you're claiming poverty as an excuse for cruelty, I can remedy that immediately. If you're claiming the Guild's laws prevent you, I have influence enough to protect you from their attention. What other reasons could you possibly have for refusing to ease a mother's suffering?"

Trapped. Amara felt the walls closing in from every direction. Refuse again, and the crowd's sympathy would turn fully against her. She could already see it in their faces, the way they looked at her as if she were a miser hoarding gold while children starved. But accept, and... she'd already seen what happened when her gift announced itself to the world.

"The laws—" she began weakly.

"Hang the laws!" Selanna's voice rang across the square. "What law is higher than a mother's love? What authority supersedes the bond between parent and child?" She turned to address the crowd directly, her words carrying the trained projection of someone accustomed to command. "Good people of Deymar, you who have buried parents and children and lovers—would you not give *everything* for one more word from those you've lost?"

The crowd's murmur grew louder, more urgent. Amara saw heads nodding, hands reaching unconsciously toward hidden treasures. Scraps of fabric, pieces of jewelry, anything that might hold the echo of the departed. The desperate hunger in their faces made her stomach clench with sympathy and terror in equal measure.

"Please," she whispered, but her voice was lost in the rising tide of the crowd's emotion.

"Then it's settled." Lady Selanna's smile was sharp as a blade. "You'll come with me now, and we'll see what comfort you can provide to those who need it most."

The guards moved closer, not threatening exactly, but making their presence felt. Around the square, the crowd pressed nearer, their faces a mixture of hope and accusation that left Amara feeling like a criminal on trial.

She looked desperately toward the shadows where Caedric might be hidden, hoping for—what? Rescue? Arrest? At this point, even Guild custody might be preferable to whatever Lady Selanna had planned. But she saw no sign of black cloak or silver thread-cutter, only the hungry faces of people who believed she held the key to their deepest pain.

"I..." Amara's voice caught in her throat. "I'll come. But only to explain why I cannot help you."

"Of course." Selanna's smile widened, showing teeth like pearls. "That's all I ask—the chance to speak privately about a mother's grief."

The guards formed a loose circle around them as they walked toward the carriage, but Amara noticed they were positioned more to prevent her escape than to protect her from the crowd. The realization sent ice through her veins, but it was too late to change her mind.

As the carriage door closed behind her, she caught a glimpse of the market square—dozens of faces turned in her direction, whispering among themselves about the seamstress who could wake the dead and the grieving noble who would make her do it.

———◆———

"This way," Selanna said, her voice warm with false courtesy. She led Amara through corridors heavy with mourning cloth to a chamber that might have been beautiful once but now felt like a shrine to loss.

Black drapes covered every window, allowing only thin streams of sunlight to penetrate the gloom. Candles burned in silver holders, their flames dancing across portraits of the dead boy—Erik, she remembered Selanna calling him. Every surface held mementos: riding gloves, books marked with his annotations, a lute with strings that would never again respond to his touch.

And there, spread across a table like an offering on an altar, lay the blue silk tunic.

"Sit," Lady Selanna commanded, gesturing to a chair placed precisely before the table. As Amara reluctantly obeyed, she heard the soft click of a lock engaging. When she glanced toward the door, two guards stood outside, their shadows visible through the frosted glass.

"My lady, I told you I cannot—"

"And I told you that 'cannot' is not an acceptable answer." Selanna moved to stand beside the table, her fingers hovering over the silk without quite touching it. "My son wore this tunic to every important occasion in his short life. To his first formal dinner, to court presentations, to the harvest festival where he danced until dawn because he was so full of joy he couldn't contain it." Her voice broke slightly.

Amara could feel the whispers in the fabric even from across the room—not words, but echoes of emotion so strong they made her teeth ache. Joy, pride, the warmth of being someone's beloved son. It would be so easy to awaken those memories, to let the boy's laughter fill the room one more time.

It would also confirm every suspicion the Guild harbored while marking her as a target for every desperate soul in the kingdom.

"I'm sorry for your loss," she said carefully, "but what you're asking is forbidden by Guild law. If I were caught—"

"Caught by whom?" Selanna's laugh held bitter amusement. "The Guild? I have connections at court, influence with the merchant families, gold enough to smooth any official complications. You needn't fear their retribution while you're under my protection."

"It's not just the Guild. There are others who hunt people like me. Dangerous people."

"The Wraithstitchers, you mean?" Selanna's casual use of the name made Amara's blood run cold. "Yes, I've heard the stories. Cultists who torture souls from fabric. Terrible people, doing terrible things." She leaned forward, her voice dropping to a whisper. "But I'm not asking you to torture anyone, seamstress. I'm asking you to bring back an echo of love. Surely that's different?"

The logic was seductive, almost reasonable. What harm could there be in awakening happy memories? In letting a mother hear her son's laughter one more time? But Amara had felt the dangerous pull of that blue silk, the way its whispers wanted to become screams, memories that would spill forth like water from a broken dam until they drowned everyone in their path.

"The process is unstable," she said desperately. "Echoes don't always stay echoes. Sometimes they become something else, something that can't be controlled—"

"Then you'll control them." Selanna's voice hardened. "You'll be careful, precise, skilled in your craft. Because if you refuse..." She moved to the window, pulling aside the black drape to reveal the courtyard below. "Do you see those guards? They're under strict orders regarding your departure from this house."

The threat was delicately delivered but unmistakable. Refuse, and she would not leave House Veyra as anything more than a prisoner—or perhaps a corpse.

"This is coercion," Amara said quietly.

"This is necessity." Selanna returned to the table, her fingers finally making contact with the silk. "He's still there, still waiting. All you have to do is let him speak."

Amara closed her eyes, trying to think of alternatives. She could refuse and face the punishment Selanna had planned. She could try to awaken the tunic incorrectly, create a failure that would convince the noblewoman her gifts were unreliable. She could—

"Mother?"

The word rose from the silk like a prayer. Selanna gasped, her hands flying to her mouth, tears streaming down her face beneath the black veil.

"Mother, why are you crying?"

"Erik," she whispered, her voice breaking. "My baby, my sweet boy..."

The echo was forming on its own, drawn forth by the intensity of Selanna's grief and the power locked within the fabric. Amara realized with growing horror that the choice was being taken from her. The memories wanted to wake, and only her skilled intervention could prevent them from spiraling into chaos.

She reached for her needle.

CHAPTER 10
Amara

The first stitch was always the hardest.

Amara's needle slid through the silk with practiced ease, but the moment the thread touched the fabric, power surged through her hands like lightning. The whispers that had been fragments became voices, the echoes that had been possibilities became certainties, and Erik Veyra began to speak from beyond the grave.

"Mother, I can't find my riding boots. Have you seen them?" The voice was young, bright with the casual complaint of a child whose biggest worry was missing footwear.

Selanna sobbed, pressing the sleeve of the tunic against her chest. "They're in the stable, darling. Where you always leave them."

"Oh, right. I forgot." Laughter bubbled through the silk, warm and genuine. *"I'm*

going riding with Marcus today. His father bought a new mare, and we want to see if she's faster than Lightning."

"Be careful," Selanna whispered. "Please be careful."

"I'm always careful, Mother. Well, mostly careful. Maybe sometimes careful." The laughter grew brighter, more infectious. *"Remember when I fell off Lightning into the duck pond? You were so angry, but then you started laughing too because I looked like a wet scarecrow."*

Amara felt the memory crystallizing around them, becoming more real than the chamber they sat in. She could smell the summer air, hear the splash of water, see in her mind's eye a young boy dripping with pond water while ducks protested his intrusion. The joy was so pure, so innocent, that it made her chest ache with sympathetic warmth.

But underneath that joy, she felt something else stirring. The echo was growing stronger, more complex, beginning to pull other memories from the fabric's weave. Soon it wouldn't be just one conversation but dozens, a lifetime of moments trying to crowd themselves into a single voice.

She stitched faster, trying to contain the awakening within careful bounds. But Selanna's grief was like a beacon calling to every memory the boy had left behind, and they answered with growing urgency.

"Mother, why do you look so sad?"

"I'm not sad, darling. I'm just... tired."

"You're always tired these days. Ever since Father died. But you still smile for me, don't you? Even when it hurts?"

Selanna's composure shattered entirely. She fell to her knees beside the table, clutching the sleeve with desperate hands. "Yes, baby. I always smile for you. I'll always smile for you."

"Good. Because smiles are like sunlight—they make everything better. That's what you taught me, remember?"

The memory was shifting, growing darker. Amara could feel it pulling away from childhood innocence toward the final moments, toward the river and the struggling horse and the decision that had cost Erik his life. She tried to guide her stitches away from that darkness, but the echo had developed momentum of its own.

"Mother? Why is it so cold? The water's so cold, and I can't... I can't..."

"No!" Amara jerked her needle away from the fabric, but it was too late. The echo had found the memory of dying, and now it clung to that pain like a drowning man to driftwood.

"I can't breathe, Mother. The water is in my lungs, and I can't breathe, and it hurts so much..."

The voice that had been bright with laughter now screamed with terror and pain. The fabric writhed in Selanna's hands as if something living moved within its threads, and the temperature in the room plummeted until their breath came out as visible clouds.

Amara grabbed the tunic, her fingers flying as she tried to cut through the stitches that had awakened the nightmare. But each thread she severed seemed to spawn two more, and the echo grew louder, more desperate.

"Save me, Mother! Please save me! I don't want to die!"

"Erik!" Selanna screamed, clutching the fabric as if she could physically pull her son back from death. "Come back to me! Don't leave me again!"

Her desperation fed the echo, making it stronger, more real. Shadows began to move around the chamber without any source to cast them, and the candles flickered as if touched by unfelt wind. This was what Amara had feared—the moment when memory became something more, when the echo of the dead began to pull life from the living.

She pressed her palm flat against the silk and poured her will into the fabric, forcing the awakened memories back into dormancy. The effort was like trying to hold back a flooding river with her bare hands, and she felt something inside her chest tear loose like a snapping cable.

Blood ran from her nose, hot and thick. Her vision blurred, and the needle slipped from her numb fingers. But slowly, gradually, the screaming faded to whispers, then to silence.

When it was over, Amara sagged in her chair, her entire body shaking with exhaustion. The threadburn was worse this time—not just her fingertips but her palms, her wrists, climbing up her arms like an infection. Every use of her gift demanded payment, and this one had cost more than she could afford.

Lady Selanna knelt on the floor, still clutching the now-silent tunic, tears streaming down her face. When she looked up at Amara, her expression held equal parts gratitude and fury.

"You could have done more," she whispered. "You could have brought him back completely. You chose not to."

"That wasn't him," Amara said through lips that felt numb. "That was an echo, a reflection. The dead don't come back, my lady. They only leave shadows behind."

"Shadows are better than nothing!" Selanna's voice cracked like breaking glass. "You gave me moments, but you could have given me years. Hours of conversation, entire afternoons of his laughter. But you stopped. You chose to stop."

Amara forced herself to meet the woman's gaze, seeing the bottomless need there, the hunger that would consume everything she loved if fed even a single crumb.

"If I hadn't stopped," she said quietly, "the echo would have torn itself apart. And taken you with it."

"You don't know that. You were afraid. You let fear make you weak." Selanna stood, her grip on the tunic so tight her knuckles went white. "But I'm not afraid, seamstress. I'm desperate. And desperate people don't accept limitations."

She moved to the door, gesturing for the guards to enter. They came immediately, hands on their weapons, faces carefully neutral.

"Escort her to the guest chamber," Selanna commanded. "See that she has everything she needs to practice her craft. Food, water, fabric, thread. Everything except freedom to leave."

"My lady," one of the guards said carefully, "holding a citizen against their will—"

"Against their will?" Selanna's laugh held no warmth. "She came here voluntarily to help a grieving mother. Isn't that right, seamstress?"

The guards looked to Amara for confirmation. She could deny it, could claim coercion and hope they would listen. But she saw the calculation in their eyes, the way they weighed her word against their employer's gold.

"Yes," she said dully. "I came willingly."

The lie felt like ashes in her mouth, but what choice did she have? Selanna held all the power here—wealth, influence, connections that reached into every corner of the city's authority. Fighting her openly would only result in a quicker, more brutal end.

As the guards escorted her from the chamber, Selanna's voice followed like a curse: "Think carefully about what I'm offering, seamstress. Gold, protection, purpose. All I ask in return is that you use your gift as it was meant to be used—to bring comfort to those who mourn."

The guest room was luxuriously appointed but unmistakably a prison. Silk hangings covered the windows, soft carpets cushioned the floor, and a silver platter held delicate pastries and fine wine. But the windows were barred beneath their silk, the door locked from the outside, and the guards' footsteps echoed in the corridor beyond.

Amara sat at the ornate dressing table and stared at her reflection in the polished gold mirror. Blood still crusted around her nostrils, and her hands shook with the aftermath of threadburn. But it was her eyes that frightened her most—they held the emptiness that came from crossing lines that could never be uncrossed.

She'd used her gift as a weapon, turned memory into pain, brought the dead back to life just long enough to kill them again. And she'd done it not from malice or greed, but from the simple, human inability to resist a mother's grief.

"This gift will destroy me," she whispered to her reflection. "Or them."

She wasn't yet sure which outcome she preferred. But she knew with growing certainty that the choice wouldn't be hers to make. Forces were gathering around her, and she was the prize they would all fight to claim.

Outside her window, despite the silk hangings, she could see the market district where her quiet life had shattered less than a week ago. Somewhere in those twisting streets, other watchers moved through the shadows. And somewhere else, perhaps, a black-cloaked figure prepared to make choices that would determine whether she lived to see another dawn.

But for now, she sat alone with her bloodstained needle and the growing certainty that the worst was yet to come.

CHAPTER 11
Caedric

The shadows outside House Veyra's walls had become familiar territory over the past hour, each alcove and archway mapped in Caedric's memory as he maintained his vigil. He'd positioned himself across the courtyard where the ancient oak's gnarled branches provided cover while still offering clear sight lines to the manor's main windows.

He'd followed at a distance when Lady Selanna's guards escorted Amara from the market, his instincts screaming that whatever the noblewoman had planned would end badly for everyone involved. The Guild's training had taught him patience above all else—sometimes the hunt required hours of motionless watching before the prey revealed its true nature.

But this felt different. More personal. The way Amara had looked back at the market, her eyes searching the crowd, had stirred something in his chest that had nothing to do with duty or justice. She'd been afraid, not of him for once, but of the trap closing around her from other directions.

A sound drifted from the manor's upper windows—faint at first, barely audible over the evening wind. Laughter, bright and innocent, the kind that belonged to children at play. Caedric's hand moved instinctively to his thread-cutter, recognizing the supernatural quality that marked voices rising from awakened cloth.

The laughter grew clearer, more distinct, carrying words that made his blood run cold: *"Mother, why are you crying?"*

She was doing it. Right now, in that chamber, Amara was working forbidden magic under the noses of the city's authorities. Everything he'd suspected, every instinct that had screamed at him during their interrogation, was being confirmed by the ghost-child's voice floating on the night air.

The laughter shifted, became more complex, pulling other memories into its wake. Caedric found himself leaning forward, straining to hear the words that would damn her completely. But even as he listened, part of him wondered why the sound filled him with dread rather than triumph. He should be pleased—finally, definitive proof of her guilt that even the most skeptical tribunal would accept.

Instead, he felt sick.

The child's voice changed again, joy curdling into terror: *"I can't breathe, Mother. The water is in my lungs, and I can't breathe..."*

Screaming followed, raw and desperate, the kind of sound that carved itself into a listener's memory, never to be forgotten. Whatever Amara had awakened was spiraling beyond her control, dragging death-echoes from the fabric she'd been working on.

Then, abruptly, silence.

Caedric waited, counting heartbeats, watching. He couldn't see anything through the curtains, and he knew his moment had come.

The House Veyra steward answered his knock, but Caedric barely registered the man's stammered greetings. His attention was fixed on the corridor beyond, where he could see Lady Selanna speaking in urgent whispers with two of her guards.

"I require a word with Lady Selanna," he announced, pushing past the steward without waiting for permission. "Guild business."

Selanna turned as he approached, her black veil unable to hide the guilt that flashed across her features. Behind her, the guards shifted nervously, their hands moving toward their weapons before remembering who they faced.

"Unraveler," she said with forced calm. "How unexpected. Surely whatever business brings you here could have waited until morning?"

"I heard voices from your house," Caedric said bluntly. "Supernatural voices. The kind that rise from awakened cloth."

"I'm sure I don't know what you mean—"

"Where is she?"

The question cut off Selanna's protestations. Her composure cracked for just an instant, long enough for him to see the calculation beneath her grief-stricken mask.

"If you're referring to the seamstress, she's resting. The work was... taxing."

"I'll speak with her. Now."

"That's not—"

"Would you prefer I return with the full Hemlock Circle?" Caedric let the words hang between them, watching Selanna's face pale beneath her veil. "I can have this house surrounded within the hour, every room searched, every servant questioned. Or you can produce the seamstress and allow me to ask a few simple questions."

Selanna's hands clenched into fists at her sides, but after a long moment she nodded to her guards. The chamber they led him to was luxurious enough to house visiting royalty, but Caedric noticed the barred windows immediately. Whatever else this was, Amara was being held here against her will.

She sat at an ornate dressing table, her dark hair loose around her shoulders, staring at her reflection in a gold mirror. When the door opened, she looked up with eyes that looked empty, and he knew she had crossed a line that could not be ignored.

"You may go," Caedric told the guards. When they hesitated, he repeated the command with enough steel in his voice to make them reconsider their loyalty to Lady Selanna's gold.

Alone with Amara, he felt the familiar tension crackle between them—but now it was charged with knowledge that changed everything. She was no longer a suspect. She was guilty, confirmed, caught in the act of forbidden weaving.

So why did he feel more protective than triumphant?

"What did you do in there?" he asked, his voice sharper than he'd intended.

Amara's reflection met his eyes in the mirror. "I'm not sure what you mean."

"Don't. I heard it. The child's voice, the laughter, the screaming. What did you awaken?"

She turned to face him, and he saw that blood had crusted around her nostrils, that her hands shook with barely controlled tremors. Threadburn, the price all weavers paid for working beyond their limits.

"Lady Selanna forced my hand," she said quietly. "She threatened me, trapped me, made refusal impossible. What you heard was grief demanding answers that the dead can't give."

"What I heard was you practicing forbidden magic." He stepped closer, noting how she flinched despite her composed expression. "You think I can't see it? The way fabric whispers when you touch it? The careful distance you keep from anything that might betray your abilities?"

"You see what you want to see. Nothing more."

"Then explain the market. Explain Captain Thorne's voice rising from his cloak while you held the needle. Explain what I just heard."

"Fear makes people hear things that aren't there. Mass hysteria, nothing more. How many times must I tell you that?"

"Mass hysteria doesn't speak in coherent sentences. Doesn't issue military commands." Caedric leaned against the door, blocking her only exit. "You're Guild-trained, aren't you? Someone taught you to weave memory into fabric, to bind souls with thread. Who was it?"

"My grandmother taught me to mend torn cloth. Nothing more."

The deflection came too quickly, too smoothly. Caedric had heard similar denials from dozens of rogues, but none had delivered them with such practiced ease. This wasn't panic or desperation—it was skill, honed through years of keeping dangerous secrets.

"Your grandmother," he repeated. "The woman who passed down her needle and her gift. Did she teach you the limits as well? How to stop before the echoes tear themselves apart?"

Amara's hands stilled in her lap. The question had hit something vital, he could see it in the way her breath caught, the slight widening of her gold-flecked eyes.

"I don't know what you're talking about."

But her voice had lost some of its steadiness. Caedric pressed his advantage, pulling a leather glove from his belt—a soldier's glove, taken from evidence storage, known to hold strong memories of violence and death.

"If you're innocent," he said, thrusting the glove toward her, "then prove it. Hold this."

She stared at the offered glove as if it were a poisonous snake. "Why?"

"Because if you truly have no abilities beyond ordinary sewing, then touching it will mean nothing to you. Just leather and stitching."

Slowly, reluctantly, she reached for the glove. The moment her fingers made contact with the worn leather, Caedric saw her jaw clench, her eyes squeeze shut in concentration. Something stirred at the edges of his awareness—whispers trying to surface, voices beginning to wake.

Then, with visible effort, she clamped down on whatever she was feeling. The whispers died before they could fully form, pressed back into dormancy by sheer force of will. When she opened her eyes, they were bright with unshed tears and the strain of control.

"Just leather and stitching," she said, setting the glove aside with hands that still trembled.

Caedric stared at her, grudging admiration warring with professional duty. She was guilty—there was no longer any question about that. But her restraint, her careful control, suggested something far more complex than the typical rogue weaver driven by desperation or greed.

Most unlicensed practitioners he'd encountered were wild, uncontrolled, their abilities raw and dangerous. They made mistakes, left obvious evidence, betrayed themselves through arrogance. But Amara displayed the kind of disciplined skill that took years to develop, the careful precision of someone who understood exactly how dangerous her gift could be.

"If you slip," he said finally, his voice softer but no less serious, "I will be there. Don't think beauty or clever words will save you."

The admission slipped out before he could stop it, revealing more than he'd intended. Amara's eyes widened slightly, and for a moment the professional distance between them flickered like a candle in wind.

She glanced past him to where Lady Selanna stood in the doorway, her veiled figure radiating disapproval and barely contained fury. When Amara spoke, her voice was barely above a whisper. "Will you escort me outside?"

The request carried layers of meaning. She wasn't just asking for an exit—she was asking for protection, for rescue from the cage Selanna had built around her. And despite every principle of Guild training, despite the clear evidence of her guilt, Caedric found himself nodding.

"Of course."

The walk to House Veyra's main entrance passed in tense silence, Lady Selanna's objections trailing behind. Caedric ignored her protests about unfinished business and prior arrangements, his authority as an Unraveler superseding whatever agreements she'd forced from Amara.

Only when they reached the street beyond the manor's walls did he allow himself to truly look at her. In the lamplight, he could see the exhaustion etched into her features, the way her hands still trembled from whatever she'd endured in that chamber.

"Are you hurt?" The question emerged before he could consider its implications.

She shook her head. "Nothing that won't heal."

"Threadburn?"

The slight widening of her eyes told him he'd guessed correctly. Another piece of evidence in the growing file of her guilt, but somehow it felt less like triumph than concern.

"Go home," he said. "Rest. And remember—I'll be watching."

She nodded and walked away without looking back, her figure disappearing into the maze of streets that led toward the market district. Caedric remained where he was, ostensibly to ensure she didn't double back, but actually to watch for other observers.

The feeling of being watched had been growing stronger all evening, a prickling between his shoulder blades that spoke of hostile attention. As he finally turned toward the Guild Hall, movement in the shadows caught his peripheral vision.

A figure in a ragged cloak, barely visible against the building's dark stone, pulled back into an alley's mouth. Caedric spun toward the spot, his thread-cutter appearing in his hand with practiced speed, but by the time he reached the alley it was empty.

Only the lingering scent of something that made his stomach churn—old blood and decay—marked where the watcher had been standing. Wraithstitchers were close enough to observe his movements and Amara's. Which meant their interest in her abilities had moved beyond casual surveillance into active stalking.

As he made his way back through Deymar's winding streets, Caedric found his priorities shifting in ways that would have alarmed his superiors. The hunt for rogue weavers was supposed to be straightforward: identify, capture, prosecute. Clean, simple, unambiguous.

But nothing about Amara fit those categories. She was dangerous, yes, but controlled. Guilty, but principled. A threat to

Guild authority, but also a potential victim of forces far worse than bureaucratic law.

She is not the only one being hunted, he thought, remembering the shadow in the alley, the scent of death that clung to whoever had been watching them.

The Wraithstitchers were patient predators, content to observe and plan before striking. But when they finally moved, it would be with cruelty that made Guild justice seem merciful by comparison. Which raised the question that would haunt his dreams and complicate every choice he made in the days to come: when that moment arrived, would he stand with Guild law, or with the woman whose gold-flecked eyes had somehow managed to breach every defense he'd built around his heart?

The answer, he suspected, would determine not just Amara's fate, but his own.

CHAPTER 12
Amara

The basement room felt smaller than ever when Amara finally reached it, the familiar walls pressing close like the sides of a coffin. She locked the door behind her with hands that still trembled from threadburn, then slumped against the rough wood, trying to process everything that had happened in the space of a few hours.

Lady Selanna's coercion. Erik's voice rising from silk, bright with laughter that turned to screams. The feel of memories tearing themselves apart under her needle while she fought to contain what should never have been awakened. And through it all, Caedric's pale eyes watching, calculating, seeing too much.

He knows, she thought, pressing her palms against her temples where a headache was building. *He's always known. The interrogation, the tests, even letting me go—it was all just theater while he gathered proof.*

She should run. Pack her few possessions, take what coin she had, and disappear into the network of roads that led away from Deymar toward places where the Guild's reach was weaker. Other seamstresses had done it—vanished one night, leaving behind only empty rooms and whispered speculation about their fate.

But the thought of abandoning everything she'd built here, the life her grandmother had helped her create, felt like another kind of death. This basement room was more than shelter—it was the only place in the world where she could truly be herself, where the weight of watching eyes didn't press against her like a physical force.

Amara moved to her worktable, surveying the familiar chaos of threads and fabrics. Even now, exhausted and frightened, the sight of her tools brought a measure of comfort. Whatever else happened, she still had her gift, still possessed the ability to weave memory into form and give voice to the silent dead.

The scraps of fabric she'd been practicing on whispered softly in the lamplight, their stored memories stirring like sleeping animals. Each piece held a fragment of human experience, waiting for the right stitch to set it free.

She reached for her plainest needle, thinking to silence them as she had before, but stopped when she noticed something else. Newer whispers, fainter but more urgent, rising from fabric she didn't remember placing on the table. Scraps of dark cloth, roughly woven, stained with substances that made her stomach clench.

These weren't memories of joy or love or even ordinary grief. These were echoes of pain, of souls torn apart by barbed instruments, of voices that had been shredded into component threads and rewoven into patterns of agony.

Someone had been in her room. Someone had left these cursed fragments among her own work, contaminating her sanctuary with their twisted craft.

Sleep came sparingly, interrupted by dreams that felt more like visitations. Voices called to her from the darkness—some familiar, some strange, all desperate for acknowledgment. Her grandmother's lullabies mixed with Captain Thorne's commands and Erik Veyra's final, terrified gasps, creating a chorus of need that made rest impossible.

When morning light finally crept through her small window, Amara felt as if she hadn't slept at all. Her head pounded, her hands ached with residual threadburn, and the whispers from her worktable seemed louder, more insistent.

She dressed quickly and prepared to face another day of watching eyes and careful distances, but when she opened her door, she found something that made her blood run cold.

A single thread hung from her door frame, black as midnight and writhing with movement that had nothing to do with the air. When she looked closer, she could see that it wasn't ordinary fiber—it was made of something organic, twisted and braided until it resembled silk but felt wrong against the eye.

Hair. Human hair, woven with techniques that made her gift seem gentle by comparison.

Below it, on the narrow step, someone had left a bundle wrapped in oilcloth. The package was small, no larger than her palm, but it radiated malevolence like heat from a forge. When she unwrapped it with the tip of her needle, the contents made her retch.

Fabric scraps, but not like any she'd ever seen. These had been torn deliberately, their edges ragged with violence, and the threads that remained writhed like living things. Whispers rose from them immediately—not the gentle voices of natural memory, but screams compressed into fiber, agony given form and texture.

"Please... stop... it hurts... make it stop..."

The voices were barely human, distorted by whatever process had bound them into cloth. Amara could feel the suffering radiating from each scrap, the echo of souls that had been unraveled thread by thread while they still lived.

She dropped the bundle and backed away, her heart hammering against her ribs. This was a message, a demonstration of what the Wraithstitchers could do with their barbed needles and twisted craft. They weren't just watching her anymore... they were announcing themselves, declaring their interest in her abilities.

We know what you are, the display seemed to say.

Amara gathered the cursed fragments and stuffed them into her satchel. She couldn't leave them here, couldn't risk exposing anyone else to their malevolent whispers. But she couldn't destroy them either—not without proper tools, and not without risking the backlash that would come from unraveling so much concentrated suffering.

The market was out of the question. Too many eyes, too much attention, and the certainty that either the Guild or noble observers would be waiting for her next mistake. Instead, she took the back ways through Deymar's oldest quarter, following narrow alleys that wound between buildings like arteries through flesh.

She'd made it three blocks when the attack came.

They emerged from doorways, their movements that of practiced hunters. Two figures in robes that might once have been white but were now stained with substances that made Amara's stomach lurch. Their faces were hidden beneath deep hoods, but she could see their hands—pale, unnaturally long, fingers ending in nails that looked more like claws.

"Sister," the taller one hissed, his voice carrying the wet sound of something diseased. "We have been watching you. Your stitches bind whispers like no other. Such a gift should not be wasted on simple mending."

The second figure stepped closer, and Amara caught a glimpse of what lay beneath its hood—skin that looked like old parchment, eyes that held no trace of human warmth, a mouth that smiled with teeth filed to points.

"You will join us," it said in a voice that sounded like fabric tearing. "Or unravel like the rest."

They brandished their tools—needles of black iron, their points barbed with hooks designed to catch and tear, their eyes gleaming with malevolent purpose. The air around them thickened with echoes of pain and terror, the accumulated suffering of every soul they'd tortured into thread.

Amara backed away, her hand moving instinctively to the satchel that held her own needles. But these weren't ordinary rogues or desperate cultists—these were practitioners of an art that made her gift seem like child's play by comparison.

"I won't join you," she said, surprised by the steadiness of her own voice. "Find someone else for your obscene crafts."

"There is no one else," the first figure laughed. "Your abilities are unique, sister. The way you bind memory without rune-thread, the control you exercise over awakened voices—such skill could create wonders beyond your imagination."

"Wonders?" Amara's voice rose with disgust. "You torture souls into submission. You tear apart the essence of the dead and weave it into weapons. That's not wonder—that's abomination."

"Abomination?" The second figure tilted its head with predatory interest. "What do you call forcing a grieving mother to relive her child's death? What do you call summoning innocent laughter from cloth and then silencing it when it becomes inconvenient?"

The words cut through her defenses to find the guilt she'd been carrying since Lady Selanna's chamber. They were right, in their twisted way—what she'd done to Erik's memory was its own kind of violation, its own form of torture.

But that didn't make their methods any less monstrous.

"I made a mistake," she said quietly. "One I'll never repeat. But you... you make torture into art, suffering into purpose. We are not the same."

"No," the taller figure agreed, raising its barbed needle. "We are skilled. You are gifted. But gifts can be... extracted."

They moved with inhuman speed, closing the distance between them before Amara could react. She fled deeper into the alley, her feet slapping on wet stone, the sound of pursuit echoing off the narrow walls.

The alley dead-ended at a brick wall too high to climb, leaving her trapped between solid stone and the approaching cultists. Their laughter followed her, raising goosebumps along her flesh.

"Run if you like," one called. "It makes the hunt more interesting. But there is nowhere in this city beyond our reach."

Amara pressed her back against the wall, her hand diving into her satchel for anything that might serve as a weapon or shield. Her fingers found the cursed fragments they'd left on her doorstep, their whispers rising like a tide of agony.

An idea formed—desperate, dangerous, and probably fatal. But the alternative was worse.

She pulled out the tainted scraps and her sharpest needle, ignoring the way the corrupted fabric burned her skin like acid. The Wraithstitchers had woven suffering into these threads, compressed screams into fiber, but they'd made one crucial mistake—they'd used human voices, human pain, human memories.

And memory always remembered what it had been before the torture began.

Amara's needle flew through the fabric, her stitches guided not by technique but by desperate instinct. She didn't try to awaken the screams the cultists had bound into the cloth—instead, she reached deeper, toward the echoes that lay beneath the pain. The voices these souls had possessed before they were torn apart. The words they'd spoken in life, in love, in moments of simple humanity.

"I love you," whispered the first voice, freed from its cage of agony.

"Come home safe," called another, the echo of a mother's farewell to her soldier son.

"The stars are beautiful tonight," sighed a third, the memory of someone who'd found wonder in simple things.

The fragments began to glow with soft light as the deeper memories surfaced, pushing aside the torture that had been layered over them like scar tissue. Spectral hands emerged from the cloth—not the clawed weapons the Wraithstitchers had tried to create, but gentle fingers that reached toward their tormentors with something that might have been forgiveness.

"What are you doing?" the taller cultist shrieked, stumbling backward as ghostly arms encircled his waist. "Those voices are ours! We bound them, shaped them, made them into tools!"

"You tortured them," Amara gasped, blood flowing freely from her nose as the effort of undoing their work drained her strength. "But torture isn't stronger than love. Pain isn't more real than joy. And the dead remember what they were before you tried to make them into monsters."

The spectral hands pulled at the cultists' robes, not violently but with gentle insistence, as if the freed souls were trying to lead their tormentors toward some better understanding. But the Wraithstitchers recoiled from the touch, their own weapons turning to ash in their grip.

"This isn't over," the second figure snarled as they retreated. "The Guild will never protect you from what's coming. We know where you live and what you are. We will come again, and next time there will be no escape."

They melted back into the shadows like smoke dissipating in wind, leaving behind only the lingering scent of decay and the echo of their threats. Amara slumped against the wall, her legs too weak to hold her upright, watching as the spectral hands faded to wisps of silver light.

The freed souls were moving on, released from their prison of pain, finally able to find the peace that awaited beyond the veil. Their whispers grew fainter as they departed: *"Thank you... blessed... free..."*

When the last echo faded, Amara found herself alone in the alley with the ruins of her desperate defense. The fabric scraps had crumbled to ash, their stored memories finally able to rest. But the cost of freeing them had been enormous. Blood streamed from her fingertips, her vision swam with exhaustion, and she could barely keep her eyes open.

Footsteps echoed at the alley's mouth, measured and purposeful. Amara tensed, fearing the cultists' return, but the figure that emerged from the shadows wore the familiar black cloak of the Hemlock Circle.

Caedric stood in the alley's entrance, his thread-cutter drawn, his pale eyes taking in every detail of the scene. The ash that had been fabric. The lingering wisps of silver light. The blood that marked where her gift had demanded payment for its use.

His gaze fixed on her face, and she saw recognition there, understanding that stripped away every pretense they'd maintained.

"So," he said quietly. "It is true."

Amara met his eyes, too exhausted to run or lie or maintain the careful performance she'd relied on for so long. The truth stood between them, sharp and bright and impossible to ignore.

"If you think I'm the threat," she whispered, her voice barely audible, "then do what you must."

Caedric stared at her for a long moment, his thread-cutter gleaming in the dim light. She could see the conflict in his expression—duty warring with something deeper, Guild law battling against the evidence of what she'd just accomplished. She'd used forbidden magic, yes, but she'd used it to free tortured souls from their bondage, to restore mercy to those who'd been denied it.

The silence stretched between them, heavy with implications that would reshape both their worlds. When he finally spoke, his voice was gentle.

"Can you walk?"

The question wasn't what she'd expected. Not arrest, not accusation, not the cold recitation of charges that would seal her fate. Just concern, practical and immediate, as if her wellbeing mattered more than the evidence of her guilt.

For the first time since this nightmare began, Amara realized that the Guild's hunter might be her only shield against something far worse. The Wraithstitchers had made their intentions clear—they would come for her, and when they did, her choices would be submission or death… unless she had an ally who understood the true nature of the threat they all faced.

"I can walk," she said, accepting the hand he offered to help her stand. "But I don't know where to go."

Caedric's grip was warm and steady, an anchor in the storm that her life had become. When he looked at her, she saw not the cold assessment of a Guild enforcer, but the concern of a man whose world had been shaken.

"Neither do I," he admitted. "But we'll figure it out together."

CHAPTER 13
Caedric

The Guild Hall's iron gates felt heavier than usual as Caedric pushed through them, each step echoing against the stones that had absorbed centuries of secrets. Behind him, the city continued its evening routines—merchants closing stalls, families gathering for dinner, children playing in streets that would soon empty for the night. Normal life, proceeding as if the world hadn't just shifted on its axis.

He'd left Amara at his quarters three streets over, the small apartment above a baker's shop that served as his refuge from Guild politics and ceremonial duties. The wards he'd stitched into the walls would hold against most supernatural threats, including the Wraithstitchers' corrupted influence. She would be safe there, at least for now.

The question was whether she would still be safe after he delivered his report.

Caedric paused in the Hall's main corridor, studying the crossed thread-cutters carved into the stone walls. Seven years of service, seven years of unquestioning loyalty to the principles those symbols represented. Justice. Order. The careful balance that kept magical power from consuming the realm in chaos.

But what was justice when the accused had used forbidden magic to free tortured souls? What was order when the system designed to protect innocents might claim them as prizes instead?

I could omit what I saw, he thought. *Report the Wraithstitcher attack but leave out the spectral defense. Call it Guild intervention that drove them off.*

The lie would be simple, neat, believable. It would also be treason—the first time in his career that duty and conscience had demanded different choices.

He touched the thread-cutter at his belt, feeling its familiar weight. Everything he was, everything he'd built his identity around, was wrapped up in service to the Guild's mission. But that mission felt less clear now, tainted by the hunger he'd seen in Needlewarden Thessa's eyes when she spoke of claiming magical gifts rather than simply controlling them.

A bell tolled from the Hall's tower, marking the hour when reports were due. Caedric squared his shoulders and walked deeper into the maze of corridors that led to the chambers where his superiors waited.

The Pattern Council met in a room that felt more like a temple than an office. Tapestries covered every wall, their threads worked with silver sigils that pulsed with contained power. At the chamber's center, five chairs were arranged in a pentagon, each one occupied by a figure whose rank exceeded his own by decades of authority.

Needlewarden Korren sat directly across from where Caedric had been instructed to stand, his pale eyes reflecting lamplight like mirrors. To his left, Threadmistress Valeria studied a sheaf of documents with the detached interest of someone reviewing grocery lists. To his right, Master Weaver

Aldrich cleaned his spectacles with movements that suggested barely controlled impatience.

The other two members of the council remained partially shadowed, their faces hidden beneath deep hoods. But Caedric recognized the stillness that marked senior Guild members—the kind of motionless attention that came from years of hunting dangerous prey.

"Report," Korren said without preamble.

Caedric had rehearsed this moment during the walk from his quarters, choosing each word for its precision and necessary ambiguity. But now, faced with five pairs of eyes that seemed to see through flesh to the thoughts beneath, careful preparation felt inadequate.

"I followed the seamstress Amara Souster after her encounter at House Veyra," he began. "Intelligence suggested possible Wraithstitcher interest in her activities."

"Intelligence you gathered how?" Threadmistress Valeria asked, her voice carrying the chill reserved for subordinates who might have overstepped their authority.

"Direct observation. I witnessed figures in dark robes watching House Veyra during the seamstress's visit. When they departed, they left traces of corrupted weaving—hair-thread and tainted fabric designed to provoke supernatural response."

Master Weaver Aldrich leaned forward, his freshly cleaned spectacles catching the light. "And did they achieve the response they sought?"

Here was the moment of choice. Truth or protection, duty or conscience. Caedric met each council member's gaze in turn, then made his decision.

"Yes. The cultists ambushed the seamstress in an alley. Two practitioners, armed with barbed instruments, intent on capture rather than immediate termination."

"Go on," Korren prompted.

"The seamstress defended herself using unlicensed weaving techniques. She awakened spectral manifestations from fabric scraps—defensive constructs that forced the cultists to retreat."

Silence followed. Caedric had expected shock, outrage, immediate demands for arrest and tribunal. Instead, the council exchanged glances that suggested shared knowledge, careful planning, outcomes that had been anticipated and prepared for.

"Spectral manifestations," one of the hooded figures repeated. "You observed this directly?"

"Yes."

"And you're certain she was able to command and dismiss the constructs at will?" Threadmistress Valeria asked.

"She demonstrated precise control over the awakened memories. The spectral forms followed her intent, then dissipated when their purpose was complete."

Master Weaver Aldrich made notes on parchment, his quill moving with the quick efficiency of someone accustomed to recording data. "What was the nature of the fabric she used? Rune-threaded silk? Sanctified cotton? Ceremonial wool?"

"Common cloth scraps. The constructs appeared to be powered by the seamstress's ability alone, without external enhancement."

The note-taking stopped. Aldrich looked up sharply, and Caedric caught a glimpse of something that might have been hunger in the old man's eyes.

"Without rune-thread?" Korren's voice carried a note of disbelief. "You're certain?"

"I am."

The council members exchanged another round of meaningful glances. Caedric felt increasingly like an actor who'd been given only half a script, expected to play his role while the true drama unfolded around him.

"This presents interesting possibilities," Threadmistress Valeria said finally. "A practitioner capable of binding memory without Guild-sanctioned materials could be... valuable."

"Valuable to whom?" Caedric asked, though he suspected he already knew the answer.

"To the realm's stability," Korren replied smoothly. "Magical gifts of such rarity shouldn't be allowed to fall into unauthorized hands. Better that they serve the greater good under proper supervision."

The language was familiar—the same phrases used to justify confiscating magical artifacts, conscripting talented individuals, claiming resources in the name of public safety. But hearing it applied to Amara made something cold settle in Caedric's chest.

"What are your orders?" he asked.

The hooded figure on Korren's left leaned forward. "Bring her in. Alive and unharmed. We'll need time to evaluate the full extent of her capabilities before determining appropriate placement."

"Placement?"

"Within Guild structure," Master Weaver Aldrich explained. "Someone with her abilities could serve the realm in various capacities. Border defense, criminal investigation, diplomatic intelligence. The specifics will depend on her aptitude and... cooperation."

Caedric heard the careful pause before that final word, recognizing the unspoken alternatives it implied. Cooperation would be encouraged, certainly. But if encouragement failed, other methods would be employed.

"She may resist," he said carefully. "Her experiences with Guild authority haven't been... positive."

"Then you'll need to be persuasive," Korren smiled. "Explain the benefits of voluntary service over forced conscription. Emphasize the protection we can offer from cultist interest."

"And if persuasion fails?"

The smile widened. "I'm sure it won't. You've always been remarkably effective at bringing in reluctant subjects."

The dismissal was clear. Caedric bowed with mechanical precision and retreated from the chamber, but their words haunted him: *valuable... placement... cooperation... forced conscription.*

He'd spent seven years believing the Guild represented order against chaos, justice against corruption, protection against those who would abuse power for selfish ends. But the conversation he'd just witnessed sounded disturbingly similar to ones he imagined taking place in Wraithstitcher sanctuaries, where human beings were reduced to components in larger designs.

His quarters felt constricted when he returned, cramped by the weight of decisions that would reshape everything he'd built his identity around. Caedric sat at his narrow desk and stared at the thread-cutter lying before him—the symbol of his oath, the tool of his trade, the physical manifestation of seven years of devotion to Guild principles.

Bring her in. Alive and unharmed.

Simple orders, clearly delivered, backed by institutional authority that brooked no disobedience. He should be planning approach strategies, considering how to overcome her defenses, preparing restraints that would contain her abilities during transport.

Instead, he found himself remembering the terror in her eyes when the cultists cornered her. The desperate courage she'd shown in defending herself with forbidden magic. The way she'd freed tortured souls from their prison of pain, restoring mercy to those who'd been denied it.

If you think I'm the threat, then do what you must.

Her words echoed in his memory, spoken with the resigned dignity of someone who'd accepted that the world would never offer her justice, only the choice of which oppressor would claim her.

But what if she was wrong? What if there was a third option, one that didn't require her submission to either Guild or cult?

Caedric stood and moved to his single window, looking out at the city that spread below like a map of possibilities. Amara waited in his apartment, probably expecting betrayal, preparing for flight or final resistance.

She would run if she knew what the Guild had planned. Disappear into the network of roads that led to kingdoms beyond their immediate reach, assuming she could stay ahead of the hunting parties they would inevitably send. Most rogues who fled were captured within weeks, brought back in chains to face tribunals that offered only the illusion of justice.

But Amara wasn't most rogues. Her control, her precision, her fundamental decency—these marked her as something rarer than mere magical talent. The Guild would claim her abilities, certainly. The question was whether they would destroy her humanity in the process.

Better she serve the Guild than the Wraithstitchers, Korren had said. But better still if she served neither—if she remained free to use her gifts as conscience dictated rather than institutional mandate.

The thought was treasonous, but it felt more honest than anything he'd considered in years.

Caedric returned to his desk and picked up the thread-cutter, feeling its weight in his palm. Seven years of service, seven years of unquestioning obedience, all focused on this moment when duty and conscience demanded different choices.

He would follow his orders. But on his own terms, in his own time, according to his own judgment of what justice required.

The Guild could claim her eventually—he wasn't naive enough to believe he could protect her forever. But he could ensure that when that moment came, it would be because she chose cooperation rather than because she'd been denied all other options.

The Guild may think she belongs to them, he thought, sliding the thread-cutter back into its sheath. *The cult may think she belongs to them. But I will let her decide where her fate lies.*

Outside his window, the city settled into uneasy darkness. For tonight, at least, Amara would sleep safely in warded walls, guarded by someone who had finally learned the difference between following orders and serving justice.

Tomorrow would bring new choices, new conflicts, new tests of where his true loyalty lay. But Caedric found himself looking forward to those challenges rather than dreading them.

For the first time in seven years, he felt like he was fighting for something that mattered.

CHAPTER 14
Amara

Caedric's apartment occupied the upper floor of a baker's shop, its windows offering views of cobblestone streets where normal people lived normal lives. The scent of rising bread drifted up from below, warm and comforting, a reminder that outside of her growing nightmare, the world continued its normal rhythm of simple human needs.

But Amara couldn't find comfort in that normalcy. Every surface in the room seemed to whisper—the wool blankets, the cotton curtains, even the wooden table that held traces of the countless meals eaten upon it. Her confrontation with the Wraithstitchers had left her senses raw, heightened to the point where fabric memories pressed against her consciousness like voices demanding attention.

She sat at Caedric's small desk, fumbling with a needle and thread, her trembling fingers betraying her with each failed attempt to guide the cotton through the eye. The simple task that had once brought peace now felt impossible. Each time her fingertips touched the cotton thread, whispers rose from its fibers—fragments of the fields where it grew, the mills where it was spun, the shops where it was sold.

Too much, she thought, setting the needle aside before the voices could overwhelm her completely. *The attack left me open, vulnerable. I can't shut it out anymore.*

The threadburn had faded from her fingertips, but deeper exhaustion remained. Not just physical weariness, but the drain that came from using her gift beyond its natural limits. Each time she awakened memories or commanded spectral forms, something inside her stretched a little thinner, worn away like fabric rubbed against stone.

Through the window, she could see Guild banners hanging from municipal buildings, their silver thread gleaming in the afternoon sun. Somewhere behind those walls, decisions were being made about her future—whether to arrest her, recruit her, or simply eliminate the problem she represented.

The Guild, Selanna, the cult—all closing in.

The thought sent panic racing through her chest, but she forced herself to breathe slowly, evenly. Panic would accomplish nothing except to make her gift even more unstable than it already was. She needed guidance, needed someone who understood the forces arrayed against her.

Someone she could trust with the truth she'd never spoken aloud.

◆

Aella Thornfield lived in the Scribes' Quarter, where Deymar's clerks and archivists maintained the endless records that kept a city functioning. Her small house crouched between a bookbinder's shop and a mapmaker's studio, its narrow windows glowing with the warm light of someone who worked late into the evening.

Amara had known Aella since childhood—they'd played together in the market squares when their grandmothers conducted business, shared secrets and small rebellions in the way only children could. But time and circumstance had drawn them apart. Aella had found respectable work in the city archives while Amara remained in the shadows, hiding abilities that would have destroyed any chance at normal life.

The knock at Aella's door felt like crossing a threshold. Once she spoke the truth aloud, there would be no taking it back, no pretending she was just another seamstress with steady hands and an eye for detail.

Aella answered quickly, her round face brightening with genuine pleasure before concern took its place. She'd heard the rumors—everyone in the city had by now—and her expression showed the careful calculation of someone weighing friendship against prudent distance.

"Amara," she said, glancing past her toward the darkening street. "I wondered if you might come. Please, quickly—inside."

The interior of Aella's house reflected her profession: shelves lined with ledgers and scrolls, a desk covered with neat stacks of correspondence, ink stains marking surfaces where countless documents had been copied and filed. But it was also warm, lived-in, the home of someone who found contentment in order and useful work.

"Tea?" Aella asked, already moving toward her small kitchen.

"Please."

They settled at Aella's kitchen table with steaming cups between them, the familiar ritual of hospitality creating space for harder conversations. Aella had always been direct—it was what had made their childhood friendship so easy, and what made this moment so difficult.

"The whole city's talking about you," Aella said. "Thread-witch, they're calling you. Say you can wake the dead with nothing but needle and thread."

"They're not wrong."

The words emerged before Amara could second-guess them, carrying the weight of years spent in careful silence. Aella's cup paused halfway to her lips, her eyes widening with the shock of having suspicion confirmed.

"You're serious."

"I have the gift." Amara met her old friend's gaze steadily, watching fear and fascination war in Aella's expression. "I can awaken memories stored in fabric, give voice to echoes that linger in cloth. It's what my grandmother could do, though she hid it better than I have."

"The soldier's cloak in the market—that was you?"

"Yes. And Lady Selanna's son, though that... that went badly. The echo became unstable, turned from joy to terror before I could contain it."

Aella set down her cup with hands that shook slightly. "And yesterday? I heard there was trouble in Southvale Alley. Strange burns on the walls—"

"Wraithstitchers." The word tasted like poison on Amara's tongue. "They want my abilities. They cornered me, tried to take me alive so they could... harvest what I can do."

"How did you escape?"

Amara stared into her tea, seeing not brown liquid but the silver wisps that had been freed souls ascending toward whatever peace awaited beyond the veil. "I used their own weapons against them. They'd tortured voices into cloth, woven screams into fabric. I... I unraveled what they'd done, freed the souls they'd bound."

The silence stretched between them while Aella processed the implications that reached far beyond simple magical ability. When she spoke again, her voice carried the careful tone of someone treading on dangerous ground.

"The Guild knows?"

"They suspect. One of their Unravelers has been watching me, testing me. I think he saw what happened in the alley."

"Then why haven't they arrested you?"

It was the question that had haunted Amara since Caedric had helped her to safety instead of dragging her to Guild custody. The only answers she could imagine were disturbing ones.

"Maybe they want to see how far my power extends before they claim it. Maybe they think I'm more valuable as a tool than a prisoner."

Aella leaned back in her chair, her expression troubled. "The Guild's not known for leaving dangerous magic unconstrained. If they haven't moved against you yet, it's because they have plans that require you free—at least temporarily."

"What do you mean?"

"I work in the municipal archives, remember? I see the Guild's requisition orders, their personnel transfers, the budget allocations that reveal their priorities." Aella's voice dropped to a whisper. "They've been preparing for something. Increased patrols, new equipment, training programs focused on... unusual threats."

The implications settled over Amara like a shroud. She wasn't just a rogue weaver to be captured and prosecuted—she was a resource to be evaluated, tested, prepared for the conflict the Guild anticipated.

"And the Wraithstitchers?"

"They're known to target those with natural gifts," Aella said grimly. "The archives contain reports going back decades.

They don't just kill—they unravel, tear souls apart thread by thread to weave garments of horrible power. If they want you..." She didn't finish the sentence. She didn't need to.

Amara wrapped her hands around her tea cup, seeking warmth against the chill that had settled in her bones. Every path forward led to someone claiming her abilities, someone reducing her to a component in larger designs she couldn't fully understand.

"You can't stay here," Aella said quietly. "Every moment you remain in Deymar increases the chance that one of them will decide to act. The Guild will never let someone like you walk free—they can't afford to. And the Wraithstitchers..." She shuddered. "Better to die fighting than fall into their hands."

"Then what do I do? Run? Hide? Spend the rest of my life looking over my shoulder, waiting for hunters to find me?"

"I don't know." Aella's honesty was brutal but necessary. "But I know this—you can't keep running from what you are. The whispers are getting stronger, aren't they? The cost is getting higher?"

Amara nodded, unable to trust her voice.

"Then you need to learn control, real control, not just suppression. Because sooner or later, someone's going to push you past your breaking point, and when that happens..." Aella leaned forward, her voice urgent. "You need to be ready. You need to know the full extent of what you can do, not just what you're afraid to attempt."

The words hit like revelation. Amara had spent so long hiding, denying, suppressing her abilities that she'd never truly explored their limits. She could awaken memories, command spectral forms, free souls from corrupted bindings—but what else? What other applications might her gift possess that she'd never dared to discover?

"How do I learn without drawing attention?"

"Carefully. Quietly. Away from prying eyes." Aella stood and moved to a bookshelf, pulling out a slim volume bound in dark leather. "This might help. My grandmother left it to me—records of folk practices, old ways of working with memory and thread. Nothing Guild-sanctioned, but..." She handed the book to Amara with careful reverence. "Maybe there are answers here that official training doesn't provide."

Amara accepted the book, feeling its weight in her hands like a promise of knowledge she'd never dared hope for. The leather cover was unmarked, giving no hint of the secrets contained within, but when she opened it to the first page, familiar handwriting greeted her eyes.

"Your grandmother knew mine could..." she breathed.

"They learned together, I think. Before the Guild's monopoly became absolute, when practitioners still shared knowledge freely." Aella's smile held her sadness. "They hid what they had to hide, but they preserved what they could preserve. For their granddaughters, maybe, who might need it someday."

"Do you have the gift also?"

"No, thank goodness. No offense."

Outside, evening was settling over the Scribes' Quarter with the soft sounds of families gathering for dinner. Normal life, proceeding in its usual patterns while Amara held in her hands the key to understanding abilities she'd inherited but never fully claimed.

"Thank you," she said simply.

"Don't thank me yet. That book is dangerous knowledge—the kind that could get us both killed if the wrong people discover it." Aella moved to the window, peering through the curtains at the darkening street. "And I think you should go. I've seen Guild observers in this quarter more often lately. They might be watching my house."

The walk back through Deymar's twisting streets felt different than it had an hour ago. Amara still noticed the Guild banners, still caught whispers of "thread-witch" from passing conversations, still saw cloaked figures that might be watchers in the shadows between buildings. But instead of shrinking from that attention, she found herself analyzing it, measuring the threats against the knowledge she now carried.

If they come for me again, I'll be ready.

The thought surprised her with its defiance. For so long she'd been reactive, responding to crises as they developed, letting others dictate the terms of each encounter. But Aella was right. She couldn't keep running from what she was, couldn't keep suppressing abilities that grew stronger whether she acknowledged them or not.

It was time to stop hiding and start learning. Start *fighting*.

She pulled out her needle as she walked, rubbing it between steady fingers despite the whispers that rose from every scrap of fabric around her. The voices no longer felt overwhelming—they felt like resources, tools she could learn to use with precision and purpose.

She was done running. The question now was whether she would survive long enough to master what she was becoming, or whether the forces arrayed against her would claim their prize before she could fully understand the gift that made her so valuable to everyone except herself.

CHAPTER 15
Caedric

The evening air carried the scent of bread and woodsmoke as Caedric climbed the narrow stairs to his apartment, each step heavy with the weight of what he'd learned. Through the thin walls, he could hear Amara moving about—careful footsteps, the soft rustle of fabric, the quiet that came from someone trying not to draw attention.

He paused outside his own door, key in hand, remembering the spectral forms that had risen from her desperate stitching. Ghostly hands reaching out with gentle purpose, not to harm but to protect, to free souls from their prison of pain. The image haunted him more than any violence he'd witnessed in all his years of hunting rogues.

The Guild sees her as a weapon, he thought. *The cult sees her as a prize. What do I see?*

The question had no easy answer. Duty demanded he see a criminal, a threat to be contained and controlled. Training insisted she was a resource to be claimed for the greater good. But something deeper, something that spoke in his own voice rather than institutional mandate, whispered a different truth.

He saw a woman who'd used forbidden power to restore mercy to the merciless. Who'd chosen compassion over safety, justice over self-preservation. Who faced impossible choices with a courage that made his own careful adherence to rules seem cowardly by comparison.

Caedric turned the key and stepped inside.

She stood at the window, silhouetted against the lamplight from the street below. Her dark hair was loose around her shoulders, and she held herself with the stillness of someone listening for sounds that might herald danger. When she turned to face him, her gold-flecked eyes held wariness but not fear—as if she'd moved beyond terror into something harder and more dangerous.

"You followed me," she said. Not an accusation, simply a statement of fact.

"I did."

"From the market to Aella's house to here. Always watching, always calculating." She moved away from the window, her movements fluid despite the exhaustion he could see in the set of her shoulders. "Tell me, Unraveler—have you learned what you needed to know?"

The question carried layers of meaning. Had he gathered enough evidence? Formed sufficient understanding of her abilities? Decided whether she represented opportunity or threat?

"You're not hiding anymore," he said instead of answering directly.

"No point. You've seen what I can do. Half the city whispers about the thread-witch who can wake the dead." Her voice carried bitter amusement. "The only question now is who claims me first—your Guild, Lady Selanna's gold, or the Wraithstitchers' barbed needles."

"You think you can keep running? I've seen what you can do, but power without control is just destruction waiting to happen."

Something flashed across her face—anger, perhaps, or recognition of a challenge. "And what would you have me do instead? Present myself at the Guild Hall with hands bound, ready to be shaped into whatever weapon you require?"

The directness of her response caught him off guard. Most rogues, when cornered, resorted to denial or desperate bargaining. But Amara had moved past those strategies into something that felt dangerously like defiance.

"The Guild could train you. Teach you proper techniques, safe applications of your abilities—"

"The Guild could chain me." Her interruption cut through his careful phrasing like a blade through silk. "Don't insult my intelligence with talk of training and protection. I've seen how your order treats those with gifts they can't control. Conscription disguised as opportunity, servitude dressed up as service."

"You're playing with forces that could unravel reality itself. The boundary between life and death, memory and manifestation— do you have any idea how dangerous that is?"

"More dangerous than your council members who spoke of placement and forced conscription?" She stepped closer, close enough that he could see the flecks of gold in her brown eyes, the way her hands trembled slightly despite her composed voice. "Yes, I heard them. Through the walls, through the whispers that carry in thread and stone. They don't want to destroy me, Caedric. They want to use me."

The sound of his name on her lips sent an unexpected shock through his chest. Not Unraveler, not sir, but his actual name spoken with the intimacy of someone who'd seen past his professional mask to the man beneath.

"And the alternative is what? Running until the Wraithstitchers catch you? Hiding in shadows while your abilities grow stronger and less stable?" He forced steel into his voice, trying to match her directness with his own. "You awakened the dead in that alley. Not echoes, not memories—actual manifestations that could touch the physical world. Do you understand what that means?"

"It means threads remember. I only listen." Her voice softened slightly, losing some of its defensive edge. "The voices were already there, already suffering. I just... set them free."

The honesty in her words disarmed him more completely than any denial could have. She wasn't claiming ignorance or innocence—she was acknowledging her abilities while explaining the compassion that drove their use.

"It is others who demand more," she continued. "Lady Selanna wanted her son's entire essence restored, not just his memory. The Wraithstitchers want to harvest souls for their twisted crafts. Your Guild wants to turn me into a tool for the conflicts they're preparing for." She met his gaze. "But I never asked for more than I could safely give. I never tried to pull the dead fully back into life."

Caedric stared at her, recognizing the distinction she was drawing. Control versus chaos, precision versus recklessness, mercy versus exploitation. Everything he'd been trained to watch for in rogue practitioners— the signs that separated dangerous criminals from those who simply possessed abilities they'd never chosen.

He could detain her here. His thread-cutter would cut through any spectral defense she might raise, and the wards woven into his walls would prevent her from calling for help. One quick message to the Guild Hall, and within the hour she'd be in custody, ready for whatever evaluation and placement the council had in mind.

It would fulfill his oath, complete his mission, restore him to the good graces of his superiors who were beginning to question his methods. Simple, clean, unambiguous.

But as he looked at her—exhausted, defiant, ready to fight or flee but refusing to beg—he found himself remembering other moments that had shaped his understanding of justice. The Kellner farmstead, where the Wraithstitchers had tortured innocent souls into component threads. Lady Selanna's chamber, where grief had been twisted into a weapon against someone who'd tried to help. The council meeting, where human beings had been reduced to resources in larger calculations.

"Run, seamstress." The words emerged before conscious thought could stop them. "Before the Guild decides what to do with you."

Amara's eyes widened slightly, as if she hadn't expected mercy from someone who'd spent so long hunting her. "Why?"

"Because you're right. We would chain you, eventually. Maybe with silk instead of iron, maybe in chambers more comfortable than cells, but chains nonetheless." He moved to his desk, ostensibly to busy himself with paperwork but actually to avoid meeting her gaze. "And because you freed those souls in the alley. Not for gain, not for power, but because they were suffering and you had the ability to help them."

"The Guild will know you let me go."

"The Guild will know I deemed immediate capture inadvisable without proper support." His voice carried the careful neutrality he'd perfected over years of navigating institutional politics. "Wraithstitcher activity in the area, potential civilian casualties, need for additional surveillance—there are always reasons to delay when subtlety serves better than force."

She studied his profile for a long moment, and he could feel the weight of her attention like physical pressure. When she spoke again, her voice carried a note he'd never heard before—not gratitude, exactly, but something that might have been understanding.

"You're risking your career for someone you barely know."

"I'm exercising professional judgment about the best method for resolving a complex situation." The lie came easily, dressed in bureaucratic language that concealed its fundamental dishonesty. "Nothing more."

But they both knew better. This was betrayal of everything he'd been trained for, abandonment of principles he'd held sacred for seven years, choosing personal conscience over institutional duty.

And it felt more honest than anything he'd done since joining the Hemlock Circle.

Amara moved toward the door, then paused with her hand on the latch. "What happens when your superiors demand answers you can't give?"

"I'll find new answers. Or new questions." He finally looked at her, seeing the complex mixture of wariness and respect in her expression. "But that's my problem to solve."

She nodded once and slipped out into the night, leaving behind only the faint scent of fabric and the heavier weight of choices that could never be undone.

Caedric sat alone in his apartment, staring at the thread-cutter lying on his desk. Seven years of service, seven years of unquestioning loyalty, all abandoned in a moment of decision that felt more like revelation than rebellion.

He told himself he'd let her go for strategic reasons—that by shadowing her movements, he might uncover the full extent of Wraithstitcher activity in the city. That giving her freedom would reveal connections and capabilities that interrogation could never extract. That patience would serve the

Guild's interests better than premature action.

But deep inside, where duty gave way to conscience, he knew the truth was simpler and more dangerous. He couldn't bring himself to see her broken in a Guild cell, her abilities harvested for purposes she'd never chosen, her compassion transformed into a weapon against others who needed mercy more than justice.

The Guild had taught him to hunt rogues, to identify and eliminate threats to the realm's carefully maintained balance. But they'd never taught him what to do when the greatest threat came not from those who possessed dangerous abilities, but from those who would exploit them.

If she falls, he thought, touching the thread-cutter's silver blade, *I will be there.*

Out in the city, enemies roamed, seeking Amara. But for tonight, at least, she had gained an unexpected ally—someone who'd finally learned the difference between following orders and serving justice.

CHAPTER 16
Amara

The sun painted Deymar's rooftops in shades of gold and amber, and for one precious moment, Amara allowed herself to believe she might actually escape. Caedric's unexpected mercy had bought her time—hours, perhaps days before the Guild realized she'd slipped through their fingers. Enough time to gather her few possessions and disappear into the network of roads that led away from this city toward lands where her name meant nothing and her abilities were unknown.

She walked through the market district one final time, memorizing the familiar chaos of merchants hawking their wares, children darting between cart wheels, the comfortable rhythms of life continuing its ancient dance. This had been her world for many years—not perfect, often difficult, but hers in ways that mattered beyond simple ownership.

Now she was abandoning it all for the uncertain promise of freedom elsewhere.

Once an anonymous seamstress, she thought, avoiding the stares that followed her passage through the square. *Now caught between Guild law, noble schemes, and Wraithstitchers.*

The transformation felt surreal, as if she were watching someone else's life collapse while her own proceeded in comfortable obscurity. But the weight of Aella's book in her satchel, the lingering ache of threadburn in her fingertips, the way conversations died when she approached—all of it confirmed the new reality she couldn't escape.

She was marked now. Claimed by forces that saw her as a resource rather than a person, a tool rather than an individual with agency and will. The only question was whether she could outrun them long enough to find sanctuary beyond their reach.

The narrow alley that led to her basement room felt different in the daylight—smaller, more cramped, shadows falling at angles that seemed nefarious. But Amara pushed aside her unease, focusing on the task ahead. Pack her things, gather what coin she'd saved, take her needles and threads, and flee Deymar.

She was three steps from her door when they struck.

They emerged from doorways and alcoves like shadows, moving with a coordinated effort that spoke of careful planning and patient observation. Five figures in robes that might once have been white but were now stained with various substances that made her nose scrunch. Their faces were hidden beneath their hoods, but she could see their pale hands—similar to the ones she'd seen in the alley.

Wraithstitchers. Not the same ones who'd cornered her before, but others of their twisted order.

Amara reached for her needle, but one of them was faster. A length of coarse black thread whipped through the air, wrapping around her wrist. The moment it touched her skin, whispers exploded in her mind—not soft murmurs, but a chorus of torment twisted into each strand, suffering spun so tightly it had become something she could feel physically.

"Please... stop... it hurts... make it stop..."

The voices were barely human, distorted by the process had bound them into thread. They clawed at her consciousness with desperate need, begging for release from their prison of pain. But when she tried to respond, to offer the comfort she'd given to other trapped souls, the thread tightened around her wrist like a burning brand.

"Struggle all you like," one of the cultists hissed, the words bubbling through lips that glistened with something dark and viscous. "Our bindings grow stronger with resistance."

More threads whipped toward her—around her ankles, her other wrist, her throat. Each one carried the echo of tortured souls, their accumulated suffering pressing against her gift like acid against an open wound. She tried to call out, but the thread around her neck muffled her voice to barely a whisper.

"Such a prize," another cultist laughed. "The Unmaker will be pleased. A natural weaver, untrained but powerful, capable of binding without rune-thread." The hooded figure tilted its head with predatory interest. "You will serve the Great Unraveling well, sister."

Darkness closed over her as a rough cloth covered her head, but consciousness clung with desperate tenacity. Through the growing haze, she felt herself lifted, carried through twisting passages that seemed to descend deeper than the city's foundations should allow. The air grew heavy, metallic and rotten like cloth soaked in slaughterhouse runoff and left to ferment in the summer heat, while whispers rose from every surface—walls lined with fabric that sobbed with trapped voices.

When awareness finally fled entirely, her last coherent thought was a fragment of desperate prayer: *Let Caedric realize what's happened. Let someone come looking.*

But even as the thought formed, she knew how foolish it was. The Guild wanted her for their own purposes, not her safety. And a single Unraveler, no matter how skilled, would be no match for an entire cult of soul-thieves operating in their own stronghold.

————◆————

Amara woke to the sound of weeping.

Not human tears, but the sobbing of fabric itself—cloth that had been torn and rewoven with such violence that the very fibers retained memory of their violation. The sound surrounded her, pressed against her consciousness from every direction, until she realized she was lying on a floor covered with garments that twitched and whispered like living things.

She tried to sit up and discovered her hands were bound with the same black thread as before, the corrupted fibers burning her wrists while their trapped voices screamed in her mind. But the bonds were loose enough to allow movement—the cultists wanted her conscious and aware, able to appreciate the full horror of her situation.

The chamber around her was vast, its ceiling lost in shadows that moved as if they were alive. The walls were lined with hanging garments—coats, dresses, cloaks, shrouds— each one twitching faintly as if worn by invisible bodies. But these weren't ordinary clothes. They glowed with sickly light, their threads worked with patterns that hurt to look at directly, their voices raised in a chorus of suffering that made her teeth ache.

This was a trophy room, she realized with growing horror. Every garment represented a soul the Wraithstitchers had torn apart and rewoven into more useful forms. Dozens of them, perhaps hundreds, all hanging like battle flags in some commander's tent.

"Beautiful, isn't it?" The voice came from the chamber's depths, cultured and warm, carrying none of the wet decay she'd heard from the other cultists. "Each piece represents years of careful work, patient unraveling, skilled reconstruction. The collected wisdom of those who came before, preserved in thread and memory."

A figure emerged from the shadows—tall, elegant, robed in white silk that somehow remained unstained despite the corruption surrounding it. Unlike the others, this one's hood was thrown back, revealing a face that might have been handsome once but now looked like old parchment stretched over too-sharp bones.

"I am the Unmaker," he said with the formal courtesy of nobility introducing themselves at court. "And you, dear sister, are the answer to prayers I had almost stopped believing would be fulfilled."

Amara forced herself to meet his gaze, though the effort made her stomach lurch. His eyes held no trace of human warmth—just calculating interest, as if she were a particularly complex puzzle he was eager to solve.

"You're impressive," she managed, surprised by the steadiness of her own voice. "All this suffering, all this desecration, just to play dress-up with the souls of the dead."

The Unmaker's laugh was genuinely delighted. "Defiant even in captivity. How refreshing. Most who find themselves here are reduced to whimpering within minutes." He gestured at the hanging garments with pride. "But you misunderstand our work, dear sister. This isn't desecration—it's preservation. These souls would have faded into nothing, their memories lost, their essence scattered like morning mist. We've given them purpose, function, eternal service to causes greater than their small individual lives."

"You've tortured them into submission."

"We've refined them into usefulness." His voice carried the patient tone of a teacher correcting a promising but misguided student. "The process is admittedly... unpleasant. But so is the surgeon's knife, and yet we don't condemn the healer for cutting away diseased flesh."

He moved closer, close enough that she could smell the decay that clung to him like expensive perfume. When he knelt beside her, his movements carried a terrible grace, as if death itself had learned to dance.

"But you, dear sister—you could change everything. Most practitioners can only stir echoes, awaken memories that already yearn to speak. But you bind them, command them, shape them according to your will." His eyes gleamed with fanatic intensity. "With proper training, proper tools, you could create works of art that would make these crude efforts look like a child's first stitches."

"I'll never help you."

"Won't you?" The Unmaker gestured toward one of the hanging garments—a child's nightgown that glowed with soft, tortured light. "This little one fought so bravely. Held onto his memories of summer afternoons and bedtime stories even as we pulled them apart thread by thread. Shall I show you what remains of his voice?"

He produced a needle that seemed to absorb light rather than reflect it, its point barbed with hooks designed to catch and tear. When he touched it to the nightgown, the child's scream filled the chamber—raw, desperate, the sound of innocence being systematically destroyed.

Amara flinched despite her efforts at control, and the Unmaker smiled with satisfaction. "Pain is such an effective motivator, don't you think? Join us willingly, and you'll never need to hear such sounds. Refuse, and..." He gestured at the other garments, their voices rising in sympathetic agony. "Well... I'm sure you understand."

"You're monsters."

"We're artists. We work in media that others lack the vision to appreciate." He stood, the terrible needle still in his hand. "But I'm patient, dear sister. I'll give you time to consider your options, to appreciate the full scope of what we're offering."

He moved toward one of the chamber's exits, then paused. "Oh, and don't bother trying to summon your gift. The walls are lined with null-thread—any attempt to awaken the echoes around you will only drain your strength and leave you more vulnerable."

As if to demonstrate his point, Amara felt her abilities pressing against some invisible barrier, her gift sliding away like water off polished stone. The garments around her continued their whispered chorus of suffering, but she couldn't reach them, couldn't offer the mercy she'd learned to provide.

"The Guild will never save you," the Unmaker said softly. "They see you as a resource to be claimed, nothing more. But we see your true potential, the great works you could create with proper guidance." His smile was gentle, almost paternal. "You are ours now, dear sister. The only question is whether you'll serve willingly or require... encouragement."

The sound of his footsteps faded into the chamber's depths, leaving Amara alone with the tortured voices of the dead and the growing certainty that escape might be impossible. The null-thread wards pressed against her consciousness like a physical weight, while the black threads binding her wrists burned with pain.

But beneath the fear, beneath the despair that threatened to overwhelm her completely, something harder began to form. She thought of her grandmother's gentle hands teaching her to stitch, of the captain's voice rising from his cloak, of the freed souls ascending toward peace in the alley where the cultists had first tried to claim her.

I will not break, she told herself, the words taking shape like a prayer. *Not for them, not for the Guild, not for anyone who would turn my gift into their weapon.*

The garments around her continued their chorus of suffering, and she found herself listening not to their pain but to the memories that lay deeper—echoes of who these people had been before the Wraithstitchers tore them apart. A mother's lullaby preserved in a child's dress. A soldier's courage woven into his battle-torn cloak. A lover's promise stitched into silk with hands that trembled with joy.

Even here, in this place of ultimate violation, love endured. Memory persisted. The human spirit refused to be completely destroyed, no matter how skillfully it was tortured into new shapes.

I will endure. I have to. And when my chance comes, I will stitch my freedom with my own hands.

The null-thread might block her gift, the bonds might burn her skin, the cultists might think they owned her now. But they had made one crucial mistake—they'd left her conscious, aware, able to plan and hope and remember what it meant to choose mercy over power.

And mercy, she was beginning to understand, was the strongest thread of all.

CHAPTER 17
Caedric

The Guild Hall's bell tolled with the urgency reserved for crises that threatened the realm's stability. Caedric climbed the familiar stairs toward the council chambers, but each step felt heavier than before, weighted with the knowledge that his loyalties had shifted in ways his superiors couldn't suspect.

He'd spent the night staring at his ceiling, wrestling with the choice he'd made to let Amara escape. By morning, he'd almost convinced himself it was the right decision— mercy granted to someone who'd used forbidden power in service of compassion rather than conquest. But the bell's summons shattered that fragile peace, demanding accountability he wasn't prepared to provide.

Needlewarden Korren waited in the smaller briefing chamber. Beside him stood

Master Weaver Aldrich and two other senior members of the Pattern Council, their expressions carrying the gravity that preceded dangerous assignments.

"Unraveler," Korren said. "We have a situation."

Caedric took his position before the council, hands clasped behind his back in the formal posture that had become second nature over seven years of service. But inwardly, he braced for questions about Amara's disappearance, explanations for why his surveillance had failed to prevent the catastrophe had brought them here.

"The Wraithstitchers have struck again," Aldrich said, consulting a sheaf of reports. "Seven citizens missing in the past three days, including a baker's wife, two merchants, a scribe, and—"

"The seamstress," Korren finished, his gaze fixed on Caedric with uncomfortable intensity. "Your subject appears to have vanished from her lodgings sometime yesterday evening. Her possessions remain undisturbed, but there are signs of struggle in the alley behind her building."

Each word struck him like a hammer to an anvil, confirming fears Caedric hadn't wanted to acknowledge. He'd given Amara freedom, but that freedom had lasted less than a day before the cult claimed their prize.

"We've traced the disappearances to the old catacomb system beneath the merchant district," Master Weaver Aldrich continued. "Intelligence suggests the Wraithstitchers have established a primary sanctuary there, beyond casual detection but accessible for... procurement activities."

"You're to lead a strike force," Korren said. "Five Unravelers, armed with thread-cutters and sanctified restraints. Root them out, eliminate the threat, recover any surviving captives."

"Any surviving captives," Caedric repeated, noting the careful phrasing. "What about those who might not survive the rescue attempt?"

The council members' eyes met in silent communion, their slight nods and pursed lips betraying the existence of meetings held behind closed doors.

"Regrettable but sometimes necessary," Korren said smoothly. "The Wraithstitchers' work is... irreversible in many cases. Better a clean death than prolonged suffering." His voice dropped slightly. "However, if the seamstress is among the captives, she's to be taken alive. Her abilities make her valuable for ongoing Guild research."

The word 'valuable' carried weight that made Caedric's stomach clench. Not 'important' or 'necessary for justice,' but valuable—like a resource to be claimed, an asset to be exploited.

"And if she's been... compromised by their techniques?"

"Then she's to be contained until our specialists can evaluate the extent of the damage." Master Weaver Aldrich removed his spectacles and polished the lenses with quick, precise circles of his silk handkerchief, his jaw tightening with each rotation. "The Council has plans for practitioners of her caliber, regardless of their current condition."

━━━◆━━━

The entrance to the old catacomb system lay hidden beneath an abandoned church in the merchant district, its stone steps descending into darkness that seemed to swallow their lantern light. The air grew thick and stale as they descended, forcing Caedric to breathe through his mouth to avoid the metallic tang of dried blood, the sweet-sour notes of rot, and something else that whispered of corrupted magic.

Caedric looked at his fellow Unravelers. Good men, all of them, trained to follow orders and trust in the Guild's mission. They would do their duty without question, eliminate threats as directed, recover what could be recovered and write appropriate reports about what couldn't.

They would also deliver Amara to the council chambers, where her abilities would be evaluated and her future decided by people who saw her as a resource rather than a person.

I will see her free, he thought, checking his thread-cutter one final time. *The Guild will not have her.*

"Stay close," he commanded, his voice echoing off stone walls that had stood since the city's founding. "The Wraithstitchers favor ambush tactics, and these tunnels offer perfect cover for—"

The sound cut him off—a whisper that seemed to come from the walls themselves, fragments of voices woven into the very stone. Not natural echoes, but something far more disturbing: souls that had been torn apart and bound into the catacomb's structure itself.

"Please... help... can't find... so cold..."

Unraveler Kess stumbled, his face pale in the lantern light. "Sir, the voices—"

"Ignore them," Caedric ordered, though his own skin crawled at the sound. "Focus on the mission."

They pushed deeper into the maze, following signs that grew increasingly disturbing. Scraps of fabric hung from the walls like grotesque decorations, their threads still twitching with remnants of souls had been unraveled to create them. The whispers grew louder, more insistent, pressing against their consciousness like fingers seeking purchase in their minds.

And then they found the first chamber.

It might have been a burial vault once, designed to house the honored dead in peaceful rest. But the Wraithstitchers had transformed it into something obscene—a workshop where human souls were reduced to raw material. Stone slabs held partially completed garments, their threads still writhing with trapped voices. Tools of black iron hung from hooks, their barbed points gleaming with substances that made the light flicker strangely.

"Gods preserve us," Unraveler Jorik whispered, his thread-cutter trembling in his grip.

"They will," Caedric said grimly. "But first we do our part."

The attack came without warning. Shadows detached themselves from the darkness—hooded silhouettes in discolored ceremonial garb materializing from hidden recesses where the lantern light couldn't reach. But instead of the desperate resistance Caedric had expected, they fought with confidence, as if they knew they couldn't truly be stopped.

His thread-cutter sang through the air, severing spectral manifestations before they could fully form, cutting through bindings that held tortured souls in thrall to their captors. Around him, his men fought with skill, yet their eyes darted nervously to the shadows between strikes, their shoulders tensing at each ethereal wail that echoed through the catacombs.

Why did the cultists seem so unafraid? Why did they fight like people who expected protection rather than punishment?

When he cornered the last surviving Wraithstitcher, pressing his blade to the man's throat, the answer came with devastating clarity.

"You think the Guild doesn't know?" the cultist spat. "Your precious Guild supplies our thread. And when we need fresh subjects? Those same masters point us toward the forgotten ones—the beggars and orphans no one will miss."

The words rang with truth, but Caedric refused to believe it. "You're lying."

"Am I?" The cultist's laughter bubbled up like blood from a wound, sincere in its dark mirth. "How do you think we've operated for so long in the heart of Guild territory? How do you think we acquire the materials for our great work?" His eyes glittered with fanatical joy. "You're not our enemy, Unraveler. You're our leash. When the Council needs work done that official hands can't touch, they know where to find us."

Caedric's blade pressed deeper, drawing a thin line of blood.

"The Council would never—"

"The Council wants your seamstress alive," the cultist continued, ignoring him. "Not for justice, not for protection—for study. They want to understand how she binds souls without rune-thread, how she commands echoes without rune-thread. And if she won't cooperate..." His smile widened. "We have methods for extracting compliance."

The revelation shattered something fundamental in Caedric's worldview. Seven years of service, seven years of believing he served justice and order, all built on the foundation of institutional corruption that made his enemies into secret allies.

The blade sliced through the cultist's throat before conscious thought could intervene, but the damage was done. Truth had been spoken, and truth had a way of echoing long after its source was silenced.

In the sudden quiet that followed the battle, Caedric heard something that made his blood run cold: a whisper that carried Amara's voice, faint but unmistakable, drifting from deeper passages that led toward the catacomb's heart.

She was alive. Still conscious, still fighting, still refusing to surrender despite the horrors surrounding her.

"Sir!" Jorik's voice cut through his thoughts. "We need to collapse the entrance, seal them in before more escape!"

The order was tactically sound, strategically necessary. But it would also trap Amara in the depths with the cultists that remained, abandoning her to the mercy of creatures who possessed none.

Alive, if possible, Korren's voice echoed in his memory. *But if not, the cult can do what we cannot.*

Understanding dawned on him. The Guild didn't care if Amara survived the rescue, only that her abilities were contained one way or another. If the Wraithstitchers killed her, it solved their problem just as effectively as official execution.

"Begin the retreat," he commanded, watching his men prepare threads that would bring down tons of stone and earth. "Seal the primary passages."

But as they worked, Caedric made a different choice. The explosions began, and his men rushed for the surface to escape the collapsing tunnels. He turned back toward the deeper passages where Amara's voice still whispered from the darkness.

"Sir!" Kess called from the stairs. "The whole system's coming down!"

"Go," Caedric replied, not looking back. "Report the mission successful. All objectives achieved."

The lie tasted like ashes, but it bought him the time he needed. As the Guild Hall received word of the strike force's success, as his superiors congratulated themselves on eliminating the threat, he would be diving deeper into the earth, following whispers that might lead to salvation... or death.

If the Guild won't save her, he thought, plunging into tunnels that groaned with settling stone, *I will.*

Behind him, the entrance collapsed with a rumble that shook the earth above. He was alone now, cut off from the surface world and the institutional authority that defined his identity. No backup, no support, no orders to follow except the ones his conscience dictated.

For the first time in his adult life, his path was truly his own. And it led toward a woman whose gold-flecked eyes had taught him the difference between serving law and serving justice—a distinction that would either save them both or damn them together in the darkness beneath the city they'd called home.

CHAPTER 18
Amara

The chamber they brought her to was vast enough to house a cathedral, its ceiling lost in the shadows above. But instead of stained-glass windows and carved saints, the walls were draped with tapestries that made her stomach lurch with revulsion.

They weren't ordinary hangings. Each one had been woven from unraveled souls, their threads worked into patterns that shifted and writhed like living things. Faces pressed against the fabric from within—mouths open in silent screams, eyes wide with terror, hands reaching toward freedom that would never come. The air itself seemed alive with whispers, thousands of fragments of voices trapped in thread, probing at the edges of her thoughts, testing her mental defenses like desperate hands searching for any crack through which to enter.

"Help us... please... so cold... can't remember... who was I..."

The voices overlapped and intertwined, creating a symphony of despair that made her teeth ache and her vision blur. Each whisper carried the echo of someone who'd been unspooled and rewoven—mothers and fathers, children and lovers, all reduced to component threads in the Wraithstitchers' grotesque masterwork.

Amara closed her eyes, trying to shut out the horror, but the voices found her anyway. They pressed against the barriers she'd built around her gift, seeking the comfort she'd always offered to trapped souls. But here, in this place of ultimate violation, her abilities felt weak and scattered, overwhelmed by the sheer magnitude of suffering that surrounded her.

I'm losing myself, she thought, feeling her resolve begin to crack under the weight of so much pain. *There are too many of them. Too much suffering. I can't help them all.*

The Unmaker stood in the chamber's center. Around him, dozens of other cultists formed concentric circles, their faces hidden beneath deep hoods, their movements synchronized.

"Behold," the Unmaker said, his voice carrying clearly through the whispered chaos, "the great work of generations. Each thread represents years of labor and skilled unraveling. The wisdom of those who came before, preserved in forms that serve purposes greater than their small, individual lives."

One of the cultists stepped forward, carrying a garment that glowed with soft light—a wedding dress that had been rewoven with threads of agony, its original joy transformed into something obscene. When the Unmaker touched it with his barbed needle, voices rose from the fabric in harmonized screaming.

"This is to be our masterpiece," he continued, ignoring the sounds of torment that filled the chamber. "A Tapestry of Silence, woven from the essence of a hundred souls, capable of muffling the cries of an entire city. But our techniques, skilled though they are, lack what is necessary for such delicate work."

His gaze fixed on Amara with hunger that made her skin crawl. "Your stitches bind echoes in ways none of us can achieve. Where we must tear and force and break, you simply... listen. And the dead answer."

"I won't help you," Amara choked.

The Unmaker gestured, and a cultist stepped forward with a smaller garment—a child's nightgown that pulsed with faint, desperate light. "This little one has been with us for three days. Still fighting, still clinging to memories of sunlit meadows. Shall I show you what remains of his voice?"

The barbed needle touched the fabric, and screaming filled the chamber—raw, desperate, the sound of innocence being systematically destroyed. But this time, instead of stopping after a demonstration, the Unmaker continued his work. The needle moved with surgical accuracy, each cut unraveling another layer of the child's essence, reducing laughter to threads of agony.

Amara watched in horror as the boy's soul was torn apart before her eyes, his memories scattered like leaves in the wind. The screaming grew fainter as less of him remained to suffer, until only whispers remained, then silence.

"Now you see what awaits all of them," the Unmaker said, setting down his needle with satisfaction. "Unless you provide the skill necessary to preserve their essence in more... useful forms."

The demonstration had the opposite effect from what he'd intended. Instead of breaking her resistance, the casual destruction of an innocent soul filled Amara with rage that burned away her fear like fire consuming parchment.

"I see what you are," she said quietly. "Monsters who mistake cruelty for craft, torture for artistry. You're not preserving anything—you're defiling the dead for your own twisted pleasure."

The Unmaker's smile widened. "Such spirit! I do so enjoy breaking the spirited ones." He gestured to his followers. "Take her to the binding chamber. Let her contemplate her choices while we prepare the materials for our great work."

They left her in a smaller chamber carved from the rock, her hands bound with the same black thread as before. But either confidence or carelessness had made them less careful this time—the bonds were tight enough to burn her skin, but loose enough to allow limited movement.

More importantly, they'd left her near a pile of discarded fabric scraps—remnants from their unraveling work that hadn't yet been processed into new forms. The pieces were small, torn, and stained with various substances. But when she looked at them with her gift, she could see the faint glimmers of essence that still clung to the fibers. Souls that hadn't been completely destroyed. Fragments of memory that the Wraithstitchers had discarded as unusable waste.

Moving carefully to avoid alerting the guards stationed outside, Amara maneuvered the scraps closer with her bound hands. The black threads around her wrists flared with pain each time she touched the fabric, but she gritted her teeth and continued working.

Her needle was gone, taken when they'd searched her, but the cultists had made one crucial mistake—they'd overlooked the thin steel pin she used to secure her hair. It wasn't much, barely longer than her finger and duller than any proper tool, but it was enough.

The first stitch was agony. The black threads binding her hands fought against any attempt to work magic, sending jolts of pain up her arms that made her vision blur. But she persevered, drawing the makeshift needle through fabric that whispered with trapped voices.

"Who... where am I... can't see..."

The voice was faint, fragmented, barely more than an echo of an echo. But it was conscious, aware, still capable of communication despite everything that had been done to it.

"I'm here," Amara whispered, her voice barely audible even to herself. "You're not alone."

"Hurts... everything hurts... what did they do to me..."

"They tried to break you. But you're still here, still yourself." Another stitch, another spike of pain from the binding threads. "What's your name?"

"Sarah... I think... had a doll... Mama made it... pink dress..."

A child. The Wraithstitchers had torn apart a little girl and discarded the pieces they couldn't use, leaving her consciousness scattered across torn fabric like seeds on barren ground.

Amara's stitches grew more precise despite the pain, guided by rage and compassion in equal measure. With each thread she drew through the cloth, Sarah's voice grew stronger, more coherent.

"The bad men... they hurt me... tore me apart... but I held on... held on to Mama's lullaby..."

"Can you help me?" Amara asked. "I need to get free, to stop them from hurting others."

"Yes... yes, I want to help... been waiting so long for someone to ask..."

The spectral form that emerged from the fabric was translucent, flickering like candlelight in the wind. But Sarah's essence was strong enough to manifest beyond the cloth, her ghostly hands reaching toward Amara's bonds with gentle determination.

"This might hurt," the child's voice warned. "The bad threads don't like being touched."

The spectral fingers closed around the black thread, and Amara screamed despite her efforts at silence. The binding fibers writhed like living serpents, their trapped voices shrieking in harmonized agony. But Sarah's touch carried something the Wraithstitchers had never possessed—mercy, offered freely without thought of reward.

The bonds began to weaken, their corrupt power unraveling in the face of innocent compassion.

But the effort was destroying Sarah's already fragmented essence. Amara could see her growing fainter, her outline becoming less distinct with each passing moment.

"Stop," she whispered urgently. "You're tearing yourself apart."

"Already torn... been torn for so long... this is what I want... to help... to matter again..."

The bonds fell away, dissolving like smoke, but Sarah's form was barely visible now, her voice fading to the barest whisper.

"Remember me... tell Mama... tell her I held on to her lullaby..."

"Sarah, no—"

But the child's essence was already dispersing, rising toward whatever peace awaited beyond the veil. Her sacrifice had freed Amara from physical bonds, but the emotional weight of it settled on her shoulders like a cloak made of guilt.

The guards realized her escape when she was already three corridors away, their shouts echoing through the maze of passages. Amara ran through tunnels that seemed to stretch endlessly in all directions, guided by whispers embedded in the walls themselves— fragments of souls that had been worked into the catacomb's very structure.

"This way... hurry... they're coming... left turn... stairs down..."

The voices of the dead became her compass, guiding her away from pursuit and toward passages the living rarely used. But the Wraithstitchers knew these tunnels better than anyone, and their supernatural senses allowed them to track her through the maze of stone and shadow.

When they cornered her at last, Amara was swaying on her feet from exhaustion, her hands bleeding from where the binding threads had been. But she wasn't helpless—not anymore.

The cultists rushed toward her with barbed needles raised, their robes billowing like the wings of carrion birds. But Amara was ready for them. She tore strips from her own dress, stitching them together with movements so rapid her hands became blurs. Blood from her wounds soaked into the fabric, carrying her essence into the weave with each stitch.

Spectral arms erupted from the cloth—not the gentle hands that had helped her escape, but the desperate strength of someone fighting for her life. They lashed out at the approaching cultists, their ghostly fingers passing through physical bodies to grasp at the souls within.

The Wraithstitchers stumbled back, their confidence shaken by an attack that bypassed flesh to strike directly at essence. But the effort had cost Amara almost everything—her vision swam with exhaustion, and she could barely stand.

More cultists were coming. She could hear their footsteps echoing through the passages, their voices raised in excitement. She'd bought herself moments, not salvation. The tunnel ahead forked in three directions, each passage disappearing into darkness that offered no promises of escape. Amara chose the middle path at random and stumbled forward, knowing that each step might be her last.

She'd made it perhaps fifty yards when her legs finally gave out, dumping her to the cold stone floor in a tangle of torn fabric and bleeding hands. The whispers in the walls grew louder, more urgent, trying to warn her of approaching danger. But she was beyond running, beyond fighting, beyond anything except the simple act of breathing.

Footsteps echoed in the passage behind her—steady, measured, getting closer with each heartbeat. Not the chaotic rush of cultists, but something more purposeful, more dangerous.

This is how it ends, she thought, closing her eyes against the inevitable. *I tried to fight them. Sarah's sacrifice won't be wasted. Someone will remember.*

But when she opened her eyes, it wasn't a Wraithstitcher who emerged from the shadows.

"Caedric," she whispered, his name leaving her lips as softly as thread slipping through a needle's eye, half gratitude, half disbelief that salvation could wear so familiar a face.

Caedric stepped into the circle of dim light cast by the lanterns on the tunnel walls, his thread-cutter gleaming silver in his hand, his pale eyes blazing with grim resolve. He looked like a man who'd passed beyond fear and doubt into something harder and more dangerous—someone who'd chosen his path and would follow it regardless of consequences.

He knelt beside her, his free hand checking for injuries while his eyes scanned the passages for signs of pursuit. "Can you walk?"

"I think so. How did you—"

"Later." He helped her to her feet, his grip strong and steady despite the obvious strain he was under. "Right now we need to—"

The sound of approaching voices cut him off—multiple cultists, their numbers impossible to determine in the acoustic maze of the tunnels. They'd found her trail, and they were closing in fast.

Caedric positioned himself between Amara and the approaching sounds, his thread-cutter held in a defensive position. His stance shifted—weight balanced on the balls of his feet, blade angled to catch the dim light, muscles coiled with the patient tension of a man who had faced death often enough to greet it like an old adversary. But she could see the calculation in his eyes—too many enemies, too few escape routes, odds that no amount of skill could overcome.

The Unmaker emerged from the shadows like a ghost, his white robes glowing with corrupt light. Behind him came dozens of other cultists, their barbed needles in hand.

"How touching," the Unmaker said. "The Guild dog comes to rescue his quarry. Tell me, Unraveler—do you think your masters will reward you for meddling in their affairs?"

Caedric's grip on his weapon tightened, but his voice remained steady. "My masters can go to hell."

The Unmaker's laughter echoed through the tunnels. "Such sentiment. But also irrelevant. You'll both serve our purposes now—the girl as raw material for our great work, and you as a cautionary tale about the wages of disobedience."

The cultists spread out in a semicircle, cutting off every escape route, their needles raised and ready. Amara felt Caedric tense beside her, preparing for a final battle against impossible odds. He didn't retreat. Didn't surrender. Didn't even seem afraid.

Instead, he planted himself firmly between her and their enemies, his blade reflecting the eerie light that emanated from the cultists' robes.

"You'll have to go through me to get to her."

CHAPTER 19
Caedric

In the dim light of the tunnel, the Wraithstichers looked like carrion birds preparing to feast. Behind him, Amara's exhaustion was obvious. She was swaying on her feet, her hands still bleeding from her escape, her gift pushed beyond its limits. But she hadn't collapsed, not yet. She stood with the same quiet defiance that had marked every encounter they'd shared.

Caedric kept his thread-cutter in guard position, the silver blade humming with contained power. The Unmaker stepped closer.

"You serve the same masters we do, whether you acknowledge it or not. Your precious Pattern Council has used us for decades—cleaning up inconvenient problems, eliminating threats that couldn't be handled through proper legal channels."

"The Guild would never—"

"The Guild made us," the Unmaker interrupted. "Every soul we've harvested, every echo we've bound, every garment we've woven—all of it approved by the very authority you've spent your life serving. You cut loose what they wouldn't bind, Unraveler. We simply gather the scraps."

The truth of it settled in Caedric's chest like a stone. Seven years of hunting rogues, seven years of believing he served justice, all built on the foundation of institutional corruption that made his enemies into secret allies. But this wasn't the time for a philosophical crisis—not with dozens of barbed needles aimed at his heart.

"Whatever the Guild may have done," he said, his voice steadier than he felt, "it doesn't make your work any less monstrous."

"Monstrous?" The Unmaker laughed. "Such a limited perspective."

The attack came without further warning. Spectral forms erupted from the cultists' garments—not the gentle echoes Amara awakened, but twisted manifestations that screamed with anguish as they clawed toward their targets. The air filled with the sound of tearing fabric and tortured voices, while barbed needles sparked with power that made the tunnel walls weep condensation.

Caedric's training took over. His thread-cutter sang, its silver blade severing spectral manifestations before they could fully form. Each cut released trapped voices in brief bursts of light, souls finally free to seek the peace awaited them.

But there were too many enemies, too many attacks coming from too many directions. For every phantom he dispersed, two more rose to take its place. The cultists pressed closer, their barbed instruments weaving patterns of binding and destruction that made the very air writhe with malevolent energy.

Behind him, he heard Amara whisper something that might have been a prayer or a curse. Then spectral hands began to emerge from scraps of fabric at her feet—not the twisted horrors the Wraithstitchers commanded, but gentle figures that moved with purposeful grace.

Amara's voice was barely audible over the battle's chaos. The ghostly figure of a young man materialized beside her, his hands raised toward the approaching nightmares. Other spirits followed—a soldier's disciplined stance, a mother's protective fury, a scholar's quiet determination. All of them fragments Amara had somehow preserved from the cultists' trophy room, echoes she'd freed and bound to new purpose.

For the first time in their strange, complicated relationship, they fought as allies. Caedric's blade carved through supernatural defenses while Amara's gift provided reinforcement and support, their abilities complementing each other with natural synchrony.

The Unmaker hadn't joined the general melee. He stood apart from his followers, working on something that made the tunnel walls crack with pressure. When he finally stepped forward, the garment he wore had transformed—no longer simple white robes, but a cloak woven from dozens of souls, their voices raised in harmonized screaming.

"Impressive display," he said, his voice somehow audible over the supernatural cacophony. "But futile. Do you know what this is, Unraveler?" He gestured at the writhing cloak. "Forty-seven souls, carefully harvested, skillfully woven into a single garment of power. Each one was a rogue weaver your Guild failed to capture—criminals whose abilities made them too dangerous to live but too valuable to simply execute."

Caedric's blade wavered as recognition struck. Some of those voices were familiar— rogues he'd hunted, practitioners who'd vanished from Guild custody under mysterious circumstances. He'd been told they'd died resisting arrest, their abilities lost to the realm forever.

Instead, they'd been delivered to these monsters for conversion into weapons.

"You begin to understand," the Unmaker continued, raising a needle that looked less like a tool and more an instrument of torture. "Your Guild creates us through its failures, feeds us through its necessities. We are not your enemy, Unraveler—we are your shadow."

The cloak of souls lashed out like a living thing, spectral arms reaching toward Caedric with desperate hunger. They were fragments of consciousness driven mad by systematic torture, their humanity burned away until only anguish remained.

Caedric met the attack with silver steel, his thread-cutter carving through ghostly flesh. But each cut revealed new horrors—memories of the practitioners these souls had been, the abilities they'd possessed, the slow agony of having their essence torn apart thread by thread.

"They trusted Guild justice," the Unmaker taunted, his needle weaving patterns that made reality bend around its point. "Believed their rights would be respected, their humanity preserved. Instead, they were delivered to us for processing. Just as you'll be delivered, Unraveler. Just as she'll be delivered."

The needle swept toward Caedric's throat, but he twisted aside, letting the barbed point scrape against his thread-cutter's guard. The impact sent shockwaves up his arm, but his grip held firm.

"I'm not part of the Guild anymore," he snarled, driving his blade toward the Unmaker's heart.

The older man flowed backward with inhuman grace, his cloak of souls writhing around him.

"No? Then what are you, fallen Unraveler? What cause do you serve now?"

The question struck him deep. What was he, if not a Guild enforcer? What purpose drove him, if not institutional loyalty? Behind him, Amara cried out in pain and effort, her spectral defenders beginning to flicker as exhaustion drained her strength. The cultists pressed closer, sensing victory.

She needs time, Caedric realized. *Time to recover, to gather strength for whatever desperate gambit she's planning.*

He hurled his body toward the Unmaker, all caution abandoned, while his sword cut an arc through the miasma of otherworldly decay that hung between them. Each strike was perfectly aimed, perfectly timed, each movement flowing into the next like water over stone—the culmination of countless hours spent bleeding on the Guild's training grounds, where mercy was considered a weakness and survival the only measure of success.

But the Unmaker was older, more experienced, his needle dancing with the skill that came from having stitched a thousand souls into the void. He turned aside Caedric's attacks with casual expertise, his cloak of souls providing defense while seeking openings for counterattack.

"You fight well," the cultist acknowledged, his needle leaving a thin line of blood across Caedric's cheek. "But you fight for nothing. No cause, no principle, no authority greater than your own confused conscience."

"I fight for her," Caedric replied, feinting toward the man's shoulder before driving his blade toward his ribs.

"For a rogue weaver? A criminal whose abilities threaten the realm's stability?" The Unmaker's laugh was genuinely delighted. "How perfectly ironic. The Guild's perfect hunter, reduced to protecting the very prey he was trained to capture."

The needle slipped past Caedric's guard, its barbed point scraping against his ribs through torn fabric. Pain flared bright and hot, but he used the momentum to trap the weapon against his body, pinning the Unmaker's arm while his own blade swept toward the man's throat.

Behind him, he heard Amara's voice rise above the battle's chaos—not words, but something deeper, more primal. A song that seemed to call forth every echo in the catacombs, every fragment of memory trapped in stone and thread.

The tunnel walls began to glow with soft light as spectral forms emerged—not just the ones she'd bound to her cause, but others, dozens of them, all the souls the Wraithstitchers had tried to claim over the decades. But these weren't twisted by torture or driven mad by systematic violation. They moved with purpose, with dignity, with the quiet strength of those who'd found peace despite everything that had been done to them.

"What—" the Unmaker began, his attention diverted by the growing supernatural manifestation.

Caedric's blade punctured through the cloak of souls, its silver edge cutting through the bindings that held tortured spirits in thrall. Light exploded from the wound, bright and clean, carrying voices raised not in agony but in gratitude as forty-seven enslaved souls finally found release.

The Unmaker screamed as his greatest weapon unraveled around him, decades of careful work dissolving in seconds. Without the cloak's protection, he was just an old man with a barbed needle, facing a trained killer with nothing left to lose.

Caedric's thread-cutter took him through the heart.

Around them, the remaining cultists broke and fled as their leader fell, their coordination shattered. Some tried to take hostages from among the freed spirits, but the ghosts simply smiled and dispersed, their purpose finally fulfilled.

The cavern shook as ancient bindings snapped, the threads that had held stone and souls in unnatural configuration finally coming undone. Chunks of rock began falling from the ceiling, while cracks spread through the walls like spider webs.

"Amara!" Caedric spun toward where she knelt among scattered fabric scraps, blood streaming from her nose and fingertips, her eyes rolled back until only the whites showed. Her gift, stretched thin across too many summoned spirits, had finally snapped like overtensioned thread.

He caught her as she collapsed, her body limp with exhaustion but her pulse steady. Around them, the freed souls began their final ascension—not the desperate flight of the tortured, but the peaceful transition of those who'd found closure.

"I told you," she whispered, her voice barely audible over the cavern's groaning collapse. "I am not the threat."

No, Caedric thought, lifting her in his arms as he stumbled toward passages that led upward, toward air that didn't reek of corruption and death. *The threat comes from those who would use such gifts, not from those who possess them.*

Behind them, the Wraithstitchers' stronghold collapsed into rubble and dust, burying decades of horror beneath tons of stone. But ahead lay dangers that made cultist needles seem simple by comparison—the institutional corruption that had created the cult in the first place, the Guild authorities who would demand answers he couldn't provide.

They emerged into night air sweet with the promise of dawn, both of them battered but alive. Caedric's ribs ached where the Unmaker's needle had found its mark, while Amara remained unconscious in his arms, her breathing shallow but steady.

For a moment, he allowed himself to hope they'd escaped cleanly. The city spread before them, its familiar streets offering the promise of sanctuary, of time to heal and plan their next move.

Then he saw the Guild soldiers waiting in formation around the catacomb entrance, their black uniforms stark against the pre-dawn darkness. At their head stood Needlewarden Korren, his eyes reflecting the torchlight as he surveyed the scene with calculating interest.

"Unraveler," Korren said, his voice carrying the satisfaction of someone whose plans had proceeded exactly as anticipated. "Excellent work. The Wraithstitcher threat has been eliminated, I trust?"

Caedric felt his blood turn to ice water. "The cult is destroyed, sir."

"And casualties among our people?"

"None, sir."

"Remarkable. Such efficiency speaks well of your training." Korren's gaze shifted to Amara's unconscious form. "And I see you've recovered our missing asset. Hand her over—the Council is eager to begin its evaluation."

Asset. Not a person, a citizen, not even a prisoner—asset, a resource to be claimed and exploited according to institutional need.

Caedric's grip on Amara tightened unconsciously. "She requires medical attention, sir. The trauma of captivity—"

"Will be addressed by Guild specialists," Korren interrupted. "Who are far better qualified to handle subjects with her particular... complications."

The soldiers moved closer, hands on their weapons, ready to enforce orders if necessary. But their positioning was careful, professional—they expected compliance, not resistance. After all, Caedric was one of them, bound by oaths that superseded personal preference.

The real battle was about to begin.

CHAPTER 20
Amara

Consciousness returned in fragments, each one sharp with pain and confusion. Stone walls lined with silver thread. Voices raised in formal debate. The weight of watching eyes pressing against her like a physical force. When awareness finally coalesced, Amara found herself in a great chamber, supported by guards whose grip was the only thing keeping her upright.

She was in the Guild Hall.

The walls rose around her like a cathedral dedicated to the worship of authority. Ancient looms lined the walls, their frames carved with sigils that pulsed with contained power. Between them hung tapestries that chronicled centuries of royal history—kings crowned and buried, wars won and lost, dynasties that had ruled the realm before fading into memory.

But these weren't ordinary hangings. Each one whispered with the voices of the dead, their threads worked with techniques that bound royal essence into cloth. She could feel them calling to her gift, begging for acknowledgment, pleading for one final chance to speak.

At the chamber's heart were five chairs arranged in a pentagon, each occupied by a member of the Pattern Council. Their robes were silver-threaded silk that reflected the torchlight like mirrors, and their eyes held the hunger of people who'd spent their lifetime accumulating power.

Needlewarden Korren sat directly across from where she stood, his pale gaze reflecting no warmth or mercy. Threadmistress Valeria sat to his left, her fingernail tracing each line of the document in front of her as if tallying bolts of cloth rather than Amara's transgressions. Master Weaver Aldrich occupied the right chair, polishing his spectacles with small circular motions that quickened as he watched the scene unfold before him.

"Amara Souster," Korren began, his voice carrying clearly through the chamber's vaulted space. "Seamstress, rogue weaver, practitioner of unlicensed magic. You stand accused of violations that carry penalties ranging from imprisonment to execution."

Amara tried to speak, but her throat felt raw from the smoke and dust of the collapsed catacombs. When words finally came, they emerged as barely more than a whisper. "What do you want from me?"

"Service," Threadmistress Valeria said simply. "Your abilities are too valuable to waste on punishment. Serve the Guild willingly, and you'll find us generous masters."

"And if I refuse?"

Master Weaver Aldrich gestured toward the chamber's shadows, where black-cloaked figures stood with thread-cutters at their belts. The Hemlock Circle, ready to carry out whatever sentence the council decreed.

"Refusal is not an option," Korren said. "Your gift belongs to the realm now. The only question is whether you'll use it in service to proper authority willingly or..." He didn't finish the sentence. He didn't need to.

Movement at the chamber's edge caught her attention. Caedric stood among the other Unravelers, his face a careful mask that revealed nothing of his thoughts. But beneath his careful mask, his body betrayed him—shoulders rigid as loom-wood, fingers hovering at his belt where his thread-cutter hung, his entire frame frozen in that unnatural quiet that precedes a storm's first lightning strike.

Will he stand with them? she wondered. *Or has everything we've shared been enough to break seven years of conditioning?*

"To demonstrate the scope of service we require," Valeria continued, "we've prepared a test of your abilities."

Two guards stepped forward, carrying between them a garment that made Amara's breath catch in her throat. It was a battle-cloak of midnight blue, its edges worked with white thread that formed the royal arms. The fabric was ancient but perfectly preserved, heavy with the essence of kings.

"Behold," Korren said with reverence that bordered on worship, "the Cloak of Kings. Worn by every ruler of this realm for three hundred years, stained with the blood of seven monarchs, imbued with their wisdom and their will."

The cloak whispered to her even from across the chamber—not with the gentle voices of common memory, but with something far more complex and dangerous. The authority of generations, the divine right of kings made manifest in thread and silk. Power that could reshape kingdoms if properly awakened.

And something else, darker and more disturbing. A hunger that had grown over centuries of absorbing royal deaths, royal ambitions, royal contempt for those who served. The cloak didn't just hold memories— it held appetites, desires that would consume anyone foolish enough to give them voice.

"You want me to awaken it," she said, understanding washing over her.

"We want you to *restore* it," Master Weaver Aldrich corrected. "To bring forth not just echoes, but presence. The wisdom of kings past, given form and voice to guide the realm through troubled times."

A revenant. They expected her to tear spirits from their rest, to stitch the unwilling dead into puppets that would dance to the Guild's commands. The challenge would be immense, requiring skills she'd barely begun to develop. But the moral cost would be incalculable—not just to the souls she'd be enslaving, but to her own essence, torn apart by channeling so much power through mortal flesh.

"I won't do it." The words emerged before conscious thought could intervene.

The council members exchanged glances.

"You will," Korren said, his tone similar to that of someone speaking to a child. "Because the alternative is immediate execution, carried out by methods that ensure your abilities die with you."

Comply or face techniques designed to prevent any posthumous manifestation of her gift, to ensure her essence was eradicated completely rather than lingering in whatever fabric might hold her memory.

Amara looked around the chamber, seeing the certainty of people who'd never been denied anything they truly wanted. They would use her until her gift burned out, then discard what remained like a tool that had outlived its usefulness.

In their arrogance, they'd overlooked something vital. They'd brought her into a chamber lined with the amassed memories of centuries, surrounded by voices that longed to speak, filled with echoes that remembered what it meant to choose honor over immorality.

"Not like this," whispered a voice from one of the royal tapestries. *"This is not what we died for."*

"The realm deserves better," added another with the wisdom of someone who'd learned the true cost of power.

"Stand, daughter. Stand and choose your own path."

The voices weren't commanding her—they were offering support, strength, the courage of those who'd faced impossible choices and found ways to remain true to themselves.

"I said no." Amara's voice carried clearly through the chamber now, strong despite her exhaustion. "I won't create monsters for you. I won't enslave the dead for your convenience."

"Then you will die," Valeria said, gesturing toward the Hemlock Circle.

But before the Unravelers could move, Amara was already in motion. Her hands collected the threads pulled from the tapestries around her, offered freely by the royal dead who'd chosen to support her defiance.

Her hairpin-turned-needle moved with desperate speed, binding fragments together following instincts honed by a lifetime of listening to what fabric wanted to become. Each stitch drew blood from her fingertips, her essence flowing into the weave along with the memories of everyone she'd tried to help.

Sarah's laughter, bright with the joy of a child who'd found peace at last. Captain Thorne's courage, steady as stone in the face of overwhelming odds. The spectral defenders who'd fought beside her in the catacombs, their honor intact despite everything that had been done to them.

And something new, something she'd never attempted before—her own memories, woven into the pattern with deliberate intent. The warmth of her grandmother's hands teaching her to stitch. The satisfaction of honest work, mending torn cloth for people who needed help. The fierce protectiveness she'd felt for every echo that had trusted her with their pain.

The tapestry that emerged was unlike anything she had ever seen. Not a tool for binding or controlling, but a shield woven from love and sacrifice and the stubborn human refusal to surrender dignity even in the face of death.

Spectral figures rose from the cloth—not as slaves or weapons, but as allies who'd chosen their own purpose. They formed a protective circle around Amara, their translucent forms glowing with soft light that made the chamber's shadows flee.

"Impossible," Master Weaver Aldrich breathed, his spectacles slipping from nerveless fingers. "She's binding active spirits without compulsion. They're choosing to manifest."

The council erupted in chaos. Some members called for immediate execution before she could complete the working she'd begun. Others demanded she be taken alive for study, her techniques analyzed and codified for Guild use. Still others simply stared in fascination at a display of power that transcended their understanding.

But the Hemlock Circle moved to stop her, their thread-cutters raised to sever the connections between Amara's tapestry and the spirits it contained. Their leader stepped forward, his blade gleaming with silver light.

Steel rang against steel as Caedric's thread-cutter intercepted the strike. His eyes blazed, his decision finally made. He had chosen between the competing claims on his conscience.

"Stand down," he commanded.

"Unraveler," the other man said carefully, "you're interfering with Guild justice."

"I'm preventing Guild atrocity." Caedric's blade remained steady, positioned between his former colleague and the woman he'd chosen to protect. "Stand down, or face the consequences."

Around them, the spectral defenders pressed closer to the remaining Unravelers, their forms growing more solid with each passing moment. Not threatening violence, but making clear their willingness to intervene if necessary.

The effort was destroying Amara. She could feel her life force flowing into the tapestry, her essence binding itself to the pattern she'd created. Blood streamed from her nose and fingertips, while her vision dimmed at the edges. The thread between her soul and her body grew thinner with each stitch, stretched beyond its capacity to hold.

Let go, whispered a voice that might have been her grandmother's. *You've done enough. Rest now.*

But she couldn't release her hold, couldn't abandon the spirits who'd trusted her with their protection. The tapestry was more than a shield now—it was a sanctuary, a place where the dead could find peace without fear of exploitation.

"Stay with us," urged Sarah's voice. *"Don't leave us alone."*

"Fight," commanded Captain Thorne. *"The battle isn't finished."*

"Live," pleaded a dozen other voices. *"Live and remember us."*

Her needle slipped from fingers that could no longer maintain their grip. The great tapestry wavered, its light beginning to fade as her strength failed. Around her, the spectral defenders flickered like candles in the wind, their forms losing cohesion as the power that sustained them weakened.

But before consciousness could flee entirely, strong arms caught her, pulling her against a chest that rose and fell with familiar rhythm. Caedric's voice, rough with emotion, graced her ears. "Stay with me. Don't you dare let go."

For the first time since her gift had manifested, Amara was not alone in bearing its weight. Someone else understood the cost, respected the choice, stood ready to share the burden she couldn't carry alone.

The chamber around them lay in ruins. Tapestries had torn loose from their moorings, ancient looms stood empty of thread, and members of the Pattern Council huddled in the corner like children hiding from thunder. The Hemlock Circle had scattered, their unity broken by Caedric's defection and the sight of power they couldn't comprehend or control.

As darkness closed over her vision, Amara felt something she'd never experienced before—not the isolation of someone hiding dangerous secrets, but the warm certainty of someone who'd found an ally willing to stand against the world if necessary.

Her last conscious thought was a fragment of wonder: *Perhaps this is what trust feels like.*

CHAPTER 21
Caedric

The Guild Hall's great chamber lay in ruins around them, its ancient majesty reduced to chaos. Tapestries hung in tatters from broken looms, their royal threads scattered across stones that still glowed with residual power from Amara's working. The air itself seemed charged with lingering echoes—whispers of the dead who'd finally found voices to speak truth instead of serving political convenience.

In the center of the devastation, Amara lay unconscious in his arms, her body wracked with tremors. Blood had dried around her nose and fingertips, while her breathing came in shallow, irregular gasps that made his chest tighten with worry.

She'd nearly died creating her tapestry of defiance. Had poured so much of herself into the weaving that the boundary between her essence and the spirits she'd called forth had blurred almost to dissolution. But she'd succeeded where the Guild's finest practitioners would have failed—not through force or coercion, but by offering sanctuary to souls that had waited centuries for someone to listen to their pain.

If I hand her over, she is good as dead, Caedric thought, studying her pale face in the chamber's eerie light. *If I leave her, she is theirs. There is only one choice left.*

Movement among the rubble drew his attention. Needlewarden Korren emerged from behind an overturned chair, his robes torn and disheveled. Behind him came other survivors—members of the Pattern Council who'd weathered the supernatural storm, Hemlock Circle enforcers whose loyalty remained unshaken despite everything they'd witnessed.

"Unraveler," Korren said, his voice cutting through the chamber like a blade. "Secure the seamstress. Her abilities are too dangerous to remain uncontrolled."

Caedric felt something cold and hard settle in his chest—not anger, which burned hot and faded quickly, but the deeper certainty that came from finally understanding where lines had to be drawn.

"She has a name," he said quietly.

"She has a function," Korren corrected. "And that function serves the realm's stability. Bind her hands, seal her voice if necessary—but bring her to the containment chambers before she awakens and attempts another display."

Around them, the surviving enforcers moved into position around them. These were men Caedric had trained with, fought beside, trusted with his life during countless dangerous missions. Their faces showed the strain of what they'd witnessed, but their loyalty to Guild authority remained absolute.

"That's an order, Unraveler," Threadmistress Valeria added, stepping out from behind a fallen pillar. Her face was pale, but her voice was strong. "Your oath demands compliance."

His oath. Seven years of service, seven years of believing he served justice and order, all crystallizing into this single moment of choice. Obey, and become complicit in enslaving someone whose only crime was using forbidden power to free tortured souls. Refuse, and abandon everything he'd built his identity around.

Caedric stood slowly, his movement careful not to disturb Amara's unconscious form. When he faced the Pattern Council, his thread-cutter was in his hand, its silver blade reflecting the chamber's unsteady light.

"No," he said simply.

The word fell into sudden silence like a stone dropped into still water. Korren's pale eyes widened with something that might have been shock—as if he were reassessing possibilities he'd thought safely eliminated.

"You're refusing a direct order from the Pattern Council?"

"I'm refusing to participate in this atrocity." Caedric's voice was calm, moved beyond doubt into certainty. "She nearly died protecting souls you would have enslaved. I won't let you claim her as a reward for that sacrifice."

"You've forgotten your place, Unraveler." Master Weaver Aldrich stepped forward, his own thread-cutter drawn, backed by two other enforcers. "Your oath is to the Guild, not to rogue practitioners who threaten everything we protect."

"My oath was to justice," Caedric replied. "But I've learned that justice and Guild policy aren't always the same thing."

The first enforcer moved quickly, his thread-cutter aimed at Caedric's throat in a strike designed to disable rather than kill. But Caedric had trained these men, knew their techniques as well as his own, and his counter was already in motion before the attack began.

Silver met silver in a shower of sparks that lit the chamber like lightning. The enforcer stumbled back, surprise clear on his face— he'd expected compliance, not resistance from someone whose loyalty had never been questioned.

"Her gift belongs to no one," Caedric said, pressing his advantage with movements honed by years of combat training. "Not to you, not to the Guild. Not to anyone."

His blade took the man through the shoulder, a precise cut that severed muscle without touching anything vital. The enforcer collapsed with a cry of pain, his weapon clattering across the stones that still hummed with supernatural resonance.

Around them, the chamber erupted into chaos, and seven years of institutional conditioning shattered against the simple human refusal to participate in evil.

The escape was a blur of silver steel and spectral light. Amara's unconscious weight in his arms made every movement awkward but not impossible. The lingering echoes from her tapestry provided unexpected assistance—not attacking his former colleagues directly, but creating enough distraction and confusion to mask his route through passages he knew better than anyone.

Some enforcers tried to follow, but hesitated when confronted by manifestations they couldn't cut or bind. Others simply watched in stunned silence as one of their most trusted members walked away from everything they thought the Guild represented.

Behind them, the great chamber burned with light that had nothing to do with flame— the collected power of centuries finally released from institutional control, free to seek whatever purpose it chose rather than serving the convenience of those who claimed authority over the dead.

———◆———

The abandoned shrine lay three miles outside of Deymar's borders, its stone walls weathered by centuries but still sound enough to provide shelter. Caedric had discovered it during one of his early assignments—a place where common folk had once come to remember their departed before the Guild's monopoly made such practices illegal.

He laid Amara on the altar with gentle care, using his cloak to cushion the stone that had been worn smooth by countless hands. In the moonlight streaming through broken windows, she looked fragile as porcelain, her dark hair spread around features marked by exhaustion and pain.

There was strength in the set of her jaw, defiance in the way her hands remained closed around invisible needles even in unconsciousness. She'd faced the Guild's full authority and refused to break, choosing dignity over survival, compassion over safety.

When she stirred briefly, her gold-flecked eyes found his face in the dim light, and his name escaped her lips like a prayer of gratitude. Then sleep claimed her again, deeper this time, the healing rest of someone who'd fought impossible odds and somehow found a way to win.

Caedric settled against the shrine's wall, keeping watch through windows that faced toward the city they'd fled. Smoke rose from the direction of the Guild Hall—whether from actual fire or lingering supernatural manifestations, he couldn't tell. But the sight filled him with grim satisfaction rather than regret.

Let them burn. Let the decades of corruption be cleansed by forces they'd tried to control but never understood. The realm would survive without Guild authority— might even thrive once freed from their monopoly on magical practice.

She nearly gave her life to free others, he thought, watching Amara's steady breathing.

While they would have enslaved her power for their own convenience.

The contrast was absolute, undeniable. Whatever dangers her abilities might represent, they paled beside the institutional corruption that sought to claim them. She used her gift to offer mercy to the suffering, while the Guild would use it to create new forms of suffering for their enemies.

Movement caught his attention—a silver gleam beside Amara's hand where her needle had fallen during the escape. But as he looked closer, he realized the light wasn't a reflection but an emanation. The simple steel tool glowed with power that seemed to pulse in rhythm with her heartbeat, as if it had absorbed something essential from years of contact with her gift.

They will come for us. He knew that with certainty. The Guild wouldn't simply accept the loss of such a valuable asset, while the surviving Wraithstitchers would eventually regroup and seek revenge for their shattered sanctuary. Both forces would hunt them across any lands that offered refuge, patient as death and twice as inevitable.

Let them come. They would find not a helpless rogue and a conflicted enforcer, but partners who'd chosen their path through fire and emerged stronger for the choosing. Caedric settled deeper against the stone wall, his thread-cutter within easy reach. Dawn was still an hour away, but when it came, it would illuminate a world where two people had rejected the categories others tried to force upon them.

They'd written their own definitions instead—not hunter and prey, not enforcer and criminal, but simply two souls who'd found each other in the darkness and chosen to face what came next together.

Behind him, Amara's breathing steadied into the deep rhythm of natural sleep, while her needle continued its gentle pulse of light—waiting, patient as hope itself, for the battles that were sure to come.

The journey continues with...
Threads of Rebellion

About the Author

Richard Fierce is a fantasy author with a passion for storytelling that dates back to his childhood. He first ventured into publishing in 2007 and hasn't looked back since. His books are filled with dragons, adventure, and the kind of epic journeys that transport readers to new worlds.

In 2000, Richard was named Poet of the Year for his poem The Darkness, and his love for literature extends beyond just writing—he co-founded the Acworth Book Festival in Georgia to help bring authors and readers together. Though he originally worked in retail, he eventually transitioned to the tech industry, balancing his career with his writing.

Richard lives in Northwest Georgia with his family and a lively mix of pets, including four dogs (huskies!). He often jokes that his house feels like a zoo, but he wouldn't have it any other way.

His love for fantasy started in high school when he was gifted a copy of *Dragons of Spring Dawning* by Margaret Weis and Tracy Hickman—a book that sparked a lifelong love for dragons and epic quests.